Introduction

First thing's first.

This is a zero judgment zone.

So when I tell you I hired a total babe as my boy's nanny…

You won't criticize my decision making skills.

There is one other thing…

Said babe is my best friend's little sis - and I don't know how the h*ll I'll be able to keep my hands off her.

It's been years since I last saw her.

And, boy is she all grown up.

Breathtaking eyes that can see right through me…

And luscious curves for days.

I can't help but think about her putting my son to bed…

Only to sneak into my room after…

For one WILD night.

I can't just betray my best friend.

She's everything that's forbidden.

And everything I need.

So I pushed her away.

Now, she's gone for good.

And so is the baby she's carrying.

Our baby.

F*ck what anyone says – I'm going after the best thing that's ever happened to me and I'm not turning back.

Chapter 1

Blake

I stared at the papers on my desk, tapping my fingers. The days seemed to be getting longer and longer, and the last place I wanted to be was in my office not giving a crap about what was going on. I turned toward the computer and looked at the time, rolling my eyes. It was early, too early, which only meant it wasn't time to leave yet. I knew it was a terrible state I was in, but it was what it was. I'd worked so hard for my company, but with everything that had happened over the past year, nothing seemed to matter anymore. I had turned into the guy I always pitied and never understood, and while that should have made me angry, it only made me more depressed.

I sighed, looking up at the open door, catching Inez, my assistant, staring at me from her desk. She raised an eyebrow and rubbed her face. She was staring at me again, something that had become a regular occurrence, especially since everything I didn't do fell on her shoulders. I should have cared about that, but unfortunately I didn't, which made it even more difficult for her to deal with. She tried to be understanding. She really did, but after a year, I couldn't blame her for getting impatient.

A year—sheesh, I still couldn't believe it had been that long since my lust for life had died out along with my deceased wife. The moment I'd heard the words that my wife was dead, everything inside of me had come to a screeching halt. There were too many surprises wrapped up in that one big event, and after that, I settled for going through the motions. The craziest part about it all? I was completely and totally aware it was happening, but I didn't know how to stop doing it. I had even gotten to where my responses to my eight-year-old son, Cooper, were generic, by the book, and plain as day. We muddled through the evenings with the same robotic motions, pushing through the hours until I could finally lay my head in the bed, take a sleeping pill, and pass out, only to start completely over the next day. It was like a gray fog that followed me everywhere, sucking the color and shine from my existence.

Inez wasn't the only one to notice. It was noticeable to everyone who knew me, especially Cooper. Every day, he watched me walk out of the bedroom in silence, grab my coffee, take a sip, fix something for breakfast for him, and then disappear until I was ready for work. Every day Cooper would sit there, waiting for me to say anything, do anything that would show I was still in there, but it never happened. He would leave for school in the same silence that we started the day with, and that would pick up when I got him from school that afternoon. I loved my son, but I didn't see the point in being that wild and crazy, happy man anymore. And I knew that made me a shitty father.

Cooper was his mother's son. He loved everything about her, acted like her, thought like her, and to be honest, had very little in common with me besides being the little boy I loved. We had done things as a family and it was always great, but once his mother was gone, there was no bridge for us, especially since I couldn't seem to get my head screwed on straight to save my own life. I was starting to think this was just how it was going to be from here on out.

My thoughts were disrupted by the sound of Inez clearing her throat. I looked up, realizing she had come into the office, and I hadn't even seen her do it. She had one eyebrow raised and my cell phone in her hand, offering it to me. I didn't want to talk to anyone, but I took it, knowing there was no way she was going to let it go. I glanced down at the screen and sighed. It was my best friend, Hollis. We had grown up together, been inseparable for years, and despite that I'd moved all the way across the country to Boston, he remained a staple in my life. He had been a huge influence in my relationship with my wife and was the best man at my wedding. Hit pretty hard by the news of her death as well, he'd been trying to get me back on my feet ever since. The grief and the heartbreak coupled together, though, were almost too much to bear, even with his constant support.

"Hey, Hollis," I said, trying to sound like I was busy.

"Don't act like you were busy," he chastised. "You know you were sitting there staring off into space, drumming your fingers on your desk."

"Inez needs to remember not to tell everyone my every motion." I looked up at her.

She smiled and shrugged her shoulders, walking away from the desk and back to hers. I shook my head and swiveled the mouse on the screen, hoping something would happen other than the constant count of unread emails popping up. But no, it was the same old thing. Maybe one day, I'd actually open them.

"Okay. We have something to talk about," Hollis said.

"Please, don't lecture me again," I said.

"Nope, not in the plans," he replied. "I realize now that no matter what words I say, you're going to keep fighting me on being a human being. So instead, I'm sending you something that'll help."

"A new soul?" I groaned.

"Better than that," Hollis said. "I'm sending my youngest sister, Aly, out there, and I don't want one single argument to come from you. You need this, and so does she."

"Okay, I'm confused," I said. "I mean, your sister can't be any older than twenty at this point. Why in the world would you send her out here to me? This isn't some weird mail order bride thing, is it?"

"No, you creepy bastard." He laughed. "Look, Aly is a smart, bright girl who's killing herself to get through college, and she needs a steady, full-time job so she can stop working twenty jobs at once. And you need a nanny for Cooper because, let's face it, the last time I was there, it looked like you were two steps away from feeding the kid frozen meals three times a day. You can afford to pay Aly and pay her well because taking care of your son is a very important job. Cooper probably misses having a woman around, someone he can at least rely on to smile at him, play with him, help him with school work, wash his clothes, and make sure his life is as fluent and happy as possible."

"I don't think I'm doing a terrible job under the circumstances," I said, slightly annoyed.

"I'm not saying you are but let me ask you a question. What circumstances?" Hollis said. "It's been an entire year, dude, and though I know the whole situation was screwed up, there still isn't any reason you can't at least try to pull your shit together. Cooper isn't the only one who needs that."

"Who else needs that?" I asked. "My assistant?"

"To be honest, probably." Hollis laughed. "You've put the company on her shoulders. With Aly there, though, you can take that back from her. You can start working again, and I don't mean just showing up. That doesn't freaking count. You need to work on your company, man, get your freaking head out of the sand. This company is running off dreams and hopes at this point, and if you don't start making moves, you're going to lose it all."

"It's not doing *that* bad," I said.

"At the moment," Hollis replied. "You have a relatively capable assistant, but eventually, her zest will run dry. You need to run your own damn company, bro."

I thought about what he was saying, trying to create some sort of argument to counterbalance the whole idea of a stranger moving into my home, but the strength it took to argue was more than I had. I pulled out a piece of paper and grabbed a pen, feeling like I had been defeated. Hollis meant the best, and maybe he was right, but that didn't break the trance I was in.

"Fine," I finally said. "When do I pick her up?"

"Yes!" Hollis celebrated. "I'm telling you, man, this is a great way to start moving forward. When the newness of it wears off, I bet you'll see how much of a good idea it is."

"Yeah, yeah," I grumbled. "What's the information?"

"You're going to pick her up on Friday from Logan Airport," Hollis said. "She's on flight 932 coming from San Francisco, arriving at ten in the morning, so don't be late picking her up. And I want *you* to pick her up, not some chauffeur. You need to get to know each other. It's been many years since you've seen her, and she's not a kid anymore."

"I'll be there," I sighed.

"Perfect, man. Well, look, I gotta run. I'll send you a text on Thursday to remind you, and cheer up, things are going to get better."

"Yeah," I said. "Thanks."

When I hung up the phone, I looked down at my screen where a message from Inez reminded me it was time to pick up Cooper. I looked up and nodded at her before standing and grabbing my jacket. I didn't want to think about it anymore, but I had to let Cooper know there'd be someone new coming into the house. It would probably be good for him, but the idea of a change from the mundane didn't sound appetizing to me at all. When I got to Cooper's school, he was waiting on the curb like usual, looking down at the ground, his coat hanging off his shoulders, and his uniform looking worse for wear after a long day at school.

"Hey man." I forced a smile as he climbed in.

"Hey," he mumbled.

"So, I have some news," I said, driving off. "I got you a nanny. She'll be here on Friday. She's going to help out around the house, get you to and from school, and whatever else nannies do."

Cooper didn't say anything, just nodded his head, looking out the front windshield. He'd turned into a small version of me, slumping through the days, not saying much, not smiling ever. He and I had very little in common and didn't talk that much. He knew I loved him, that was never a question, but between my mood and him losing his mom, he'd become a different kid. Part of that was my fault, so maybe having a nanny coming wasn't that bad of an idea after all. At least the kid would get to have a more normal existence and someone to talk to who wasn't riddled with depression and guilt.

"What are we having for dinner?" Cooper asked.

"I don't know," I said. "I was thinking about that. I think I'll make something, I'm getting tired of pizza."

"Can we not do frozen chicken nuggets, please?" Cooper begged.

I smiled slightly and nodded. I needed to pick my ass up because this kid was getting the full brunt of my incurable lassitude.

Chapter 2

Aly

It was Wednesday, the only day of the week when I worked only one of my jobs and was off by the afternoon. I really wanted to sleep, but I had a ton of school work to catch up on. There was also laundry overflowing from the baskets, and my head was not in the right place for either task. My brother, Hollis, had called earlier and told me he had something to tell me. It always made me nervous when he had some sort of surprise in store. It was never something simple. Just then, I heard him walk into my parents' house, his voice bellowing through the empty halls.

"Hello?" he said.

"I'm back here, folding laundry," I yelled out.

He popped his head around the corner. "Oh, there you are. Where is everyone?"

"Work," I said. "I gotta get dinner started so Mom doesn't have to worry about it."

"You're a regular Mary Poppins." He chuckled. "For middle-aged people."

I snorted. "Yeah, it's the least I can do for them letting me stay here while I get through school."

"Since you brought it up," Hollis said, sitting down in the chair next to the bed. "I've set something up for you."

"Oh God." I rolled my eyes. "What?"

"You're going to fly out to Boston and become Blake's son's nanny," Hollis said with a big grin.

"What?" I said, looking at him with wide eyes. "That seems a little random. I don't get it. Why would you want to ship me off to Blake's?"

"Don't be hurt. It's not like that. I'm not trying to get rid of you," he said. "It's just that he'll pay you really well, and I mean twice the amount you make at both your jobs combined."

"That's a lot of money," I said, pondering.

"Well, it's worth it," Hollis replied. "And while you're there, you can do some of your online courses for college while his son Cooper is at school. I know you've been struggling to catch up on your degree with how much you work."

"I have to work that much. You know Mom and Dad can't afford college for me," I sighed. "That's the blessing of being the youngest of five. I was kind of left to the mercy of you guys."

I laughed, showing I wasn't bitter about it but letting him know I was serious. I couldn't run off to a job if it wasn't going to be long-term. I had worked hard to get the two jobs I had, not that they were glamorous or enjoyable in the least, but they paid for my school, and that was important to me. It was all so sudden, though, and I wasn't used to sudden changes like that. My life had been relatively simple since I was a kid with two working parents and a house full of kids.

"Look, I know you've been working two full-time jobs," Hollis said, "and trying to do school work at the same time. This is actually the first time I've seen you doing something *other* than that," he said, motioning to where I sat.

"Well, I should be working on schoolwork, but Mom asked me to fold the laundry she put in this morning," I said. "You know she needs the help. They've always been hard-core in their work ethic, which is the only reason I'm surviving this routine as it is. They taught me well."

"They did." Hollis smiled. "You're one of the hardest-working people I know, but you shouldn't have to kill yourself if there's another option. I know you've been struggling to keep up with school."

I sighed. "Yeah, I had to drop another class."

"See?" Hollis said. "If you took this job with Blake, it would give you time to spend on your studies. Like, eight hours a day you could commit to it or maybe five or six if you have nanny duties to do during the day. Still, that's a hell of a lot more than you have now. On top of that, you'd be helping Blake out too. He needs something like this and so does Cooper."

"He's still not doing well since his wife died?" I asked, feeling sympathy for Hollis' best friend.

Hollis shook his head. "No, he isn't. Cooper struggles, but Blake was thrown for a loop. He can't seem to get his head back in the game, and I know his son could use someone like you in his life. The kid is lost."

I looked down at the towel I was folding, thinking about the opportunity in front of me. I felt for Blake. I couldn't imagine how it would feel to lose the love of your life. His son had to be in a very lonely place with how sad and broken-down Blake sounded. It was a huge choice to make, though, giving up everything I'd worked for here; my family, my jobs.

Still, I couldn't help feeling a tingle in my chest thinking about Blake. He had been my brother's best friend forever and when I was a kid, I'd always had a serious crush on him. There was definitely an upside to going to work every day and being around a man like him. He was successful, handsome, powerful, and even though it was a moot point, seeing as I would be his employee – and his best friend's little sister – it still made me want to jump right on the opportunity.

"Well," I said. "If it will help them and I can get my work done too, I'll do it."

"Yes!" Hollis jumped up and hugged me tightly. "I knew you would agree," Hollis whispered, still hugging me tightly. "You have a heart of gold, and your ambition is amazing."

"You should have started out with that." I laughed.

"I couldn't unleash all the good stuff right off the bat," he said. "I have to store it up and really put it out there when it counts. Otherwise, it wouldn't mean so much."

"Right. Heaven forbid you tell me how amazing I am all the time."

"Okay," he said. With a dramatic flourish, he pulled out an envelope. "Here's your plane ticket. I already bought it since I know you so well."

"You are too much," I said, shaking my head.

"And there's some cash in there in case you want some food or something," he replied with a smile.

"Thank you." I chuckled. "Or six shots of whiskey."

"I don't know if showing up drunk is a good first impression or not, but hey, everybody has their tactics."

"Well, thank you for the opportunity. I appreciate it." I smiled.

"Thank you for taking care of my best friend," Hollis replied. "Alright, I'm out of here. If you need a ride to the airport, let me know."

"Will do," I called out as he dashed from the house.

When the front door closed, I put the towel that I was folding down and laughed. That was definitely a surprise I wasn't expecting. Since the decision was made, I might as well get to packing. I was leaving on Friday, and I would need to be prepared for a move across the country. I finished up the laundry and went in the kitchen, grabbing my cell phone and calling my two jobs. They weren't very happy about me quitting with such short notice, but it was a good opportunity, and one that I couldn't pass up. After that, I headed to my room and started to pack.

I pulled out the things in my closet and started going through my clothes. What would it be like to share a house with a kid? I was the youngest; way younger than my siblings. By the time I was in middle school, I was the only child left in the house, and I had no experience living with a little kid. I had no idea what to expect. Hopefully, Cooper would take to me quickly. It was probably going to be strange for him with his mom having died only a year before, but I wanted him to feel comfortable with me and me with him too.

I was majoring in early childhood development, so the job could technically be classified as practical field work for my degree program with the extra perk of getting paid to do it. It would help me understand what kind of mindset a kid his age would have, especially going through a trying time in his life. I didn't want to treat him like a test subject by any means, but I couldn't resist wanting to learn from the experience.

I grabbed my phone and pulled up my weather app. The heat in San Francisco was winding down for fall, and if it was chilly here, I could only imagine it would be extra chilly in Boston too. I wasn't sure how long to pack for, but I didn't want to leave anything behind that I might need. It would be the first time I'd be leaving home, and not just for a vacation. I would be making Boston my home, and I'd always wanted to go there. I loved San Francisco, there was no doubt about that, but I wanted to see new places, meet new people, and I had always heard Boston had some interesting personalities.

I needed to stay the course, work hard, and get my degree finished without any major distractions. I could only hope that Blake wasn't as hot as I remembered.

Chapter 3

Blake

It felt like everyone in Boston had decided to go to Logan Airport that day. There were droves of people coming down the escalator toward the baggage claim, none of them fitting the description of Aly that I had in my mind. Cooper and I had talked about the change, about having a nanny come and live at the house, and he didn't seem very excited about it at all. I had to explain it to him in the same way I was explaining it to myself. Change was always hard, and we'd been through our fair share of the negative side of it. However, if we wanted to continue to grow, to move forward with life, we needed some positive change to happen. The nanny could possibly be that positive change we needed, someone to get us out of our rut. Cooper had just shrugged his shoulders, not really saying anything.

I wanted him to look forward to someone new in his life. It would help me find solace in moving forward, but I figured I'd have to make do and set a good example. Even in his grumpiness over the whole thing, though, he'd begrudgingly helped me clean out the guest room and make it up for Aly. Instead of using his mom's old stuff, though, we went out and bought some new linens, towels, and such so we would all feel more comfortable about a woman being back in the house. It was going to be quite a change.

I looked down at the sign I had printed at the office and then back up at the crowd. I was pretty sure she would know me by sight, but I wasn't sure I would completely recognize her. Sure, I had an image of what she looked like in my head, but it was of a fifteen-year-old girl with long gangly limbs, wild blonde hair, and dirt on her knees from playing too hard with the other kids. I had been thirty years old the last time I'd seen her. My wife and I had just gotten married, and she was pregnant with our son but not enough for even us to know yet.

I had grown up in San Francisco but went to Boston to start my company. That was where I had met my wife and where we had started our family. Things had gone well for us there and so I hadn't gone back to San Francisco very much. I was busy with work and family, and when Hollis wanted to see me, he flew out to Boston to get away from the smog for a little while. I'd gone back to San Francisco a few times, but we never went to Hollis's house. We always met out at one of our old stomping grounds, and the family and I would either stay at my parents' house or at a hotel.

Having that vision of a fifteen-year-old girl in my mind led me straight to a surprise when this gorgeous, curvy, blonde-haired babe stopped in front of me and smiled. Her lips were full, her huge blue eyes full of excitement and surprise. I stared at her for several moments, unsure whether she was even looking at me. She wore a black V-neck T-shirt, tight jeans, and tennis shoes. Every curve of her body flowed perfectly like she was created out of clay, molded meticulously. Her skin was fair and so smooth like a porcelain doll . Immediately, my heart beat faster in my chest, my throat went tight, and the heat in my body shot to my face. I stared into the girl's eyes before recognition dawned and I remembered that look. It was Aly, only she was definitely not fifteen years old anymore and definitely not that gangly teen I had last seen.

Aly was a full-grown woman, and one I could barely keep my cool in front of. She raised her eyebrows at me and chuckled, reminding me to close my mouth that I hadn't even realized had fallen open while I was staring at her in shock. It wasn't like me be rendered speechless, but it was the first time a woman had pulled this kind of response from me since I'd met my wife.

"I, uh, Aly?" I sputtered.

"It's me." She laughed, her cheeks rosy.

"I don't know why, but I was expecting a fifteen-year-old," I admitted. "I guess it's been a long time."

"That it has."

My mind was running at about a thousand miles a minute trying to process what was happening. This gorgeous woman, whose smile lit up the dark corners of my heart, was going to be living in my house. She was going to be there every morning when I woke up and every night when I went to bed. I never once, when Hollis said he was sending her, thought about having any kind of attraction to her. I never thought about having a beautiful woman only feet away from me when she was sleeping or showering or anything else that was erotically running through my man brain at the moment. I hadn't thought about it at all, and if I had, it was brief, and she didn't have a face, or body for that matter, in my thoughts. I took a deep breath and shook my head, trying to gather my wits.

"Here, let me take those," I said, picking up her suitcases. "I parked in the garage."

I turned away from her, rolling my eyes at being incapable of getting my shit together and stuttering like a twelve-year-old boy hitting puberty. I walked toward the parking garage where the SUV was parked and could feel her walking quickly behind me, trying to keep up. I opened the back of the SUV and put her suitcases in, taking her other bags from her and piling them on top.

"Thank you," she said.

We climbed into the car, and I turned it on, hitting the button on the CD player before it could start blaring out Dave Matthews, which I'd been listening to all morning for some reason. I pulled through the parking garage and stopped at the front booth to pay for parking. Then, I pulled out into the busy roadway and headed toward the house on the outskirts of the city.

"How was your flight?" I asked, unsure of what to talk about.

"It was long but good," she said. "They had a couple of in-flight movies, so I wasn't too bored."

"I hate flying. I usually get drunk and pass out."

"Yeah, well, I thought maybe you'd frown on me showing up wasted." She laughed.

"You might be right." I couldn't help but laugh. The feel of it was so foreign. "So, have you been to Boston before?"

She looked over at me. "No. I've always wanted to come here, though. The only time I've been on this coast was for a trip to Washington, DC, in my senior year of high school."

"I like DC," I said. "Nice place, but Boston is definitely different."

"I've heard." Her smile made butterflies take flight in my stomach.

Aly started talking about Washington, DC, what she did there and what she didn't like about the place. I tried hard to pay attention to what she was saying, but I was only taking in about fifty percent of it. Instead, my head was swimming with the thought that this beautiful, sexy, intelligent woman was the same gangly kid I had seen years before. I was starting to think it might have been a serious mistake on Hollis's part to send her out to me. She was not the kind of girl you could ignore. Not only did it feel like I was being drawn into that perfect body, but her personality was killer too. She was bubbly but sarcastic, a combination I found extremely attractive.

I swallowed hard and gripped the steering wheel tightly, trying to push the thoughts from my head, but every time she moved, I got a whiff of her lavender and vanilla scent and the thoughts started all over again. That reaction surprised me, and while I knew it was inappropriate, I kind of liked that those emotions were making me feel alive to the world again. It was a double-edged sword for me, a dangerous place to go. On one hand, I felt guilty for having any kind of feelings like that. I'd been married for so long, it was built into my head that I wasn't supposed to lust over any other woman. On the other hand, my wife was gone, and I was still here; struggling to find some foothold on happiness again.

I'd thought my desire for another woman had died with my wife, but it was waking inside of me out of nowhere. It was confusing but satisfying at the same time and reminded me I was still alive, I hadn't died with my wife, just that part of my life had. Still, this was the woman who was coming to help take care of my son, the woman who would be there to mentor, support, and help raise of the most important human being in my life. With her living under my roof, those feelings were going to be a problem.

Hopefully my infatuation was temporary; excitement for someone new in my life, lust for an incredibly attractive woman. We didn't know each other at all, and I had a lot more things I needed on my mind than getting my nanny in bed.

Chapter 4

Aly

"I liked the Washington Monument, and the art museums were the best," I said. "What I liked most, though, was the dang food. They had the best pizza I've ever had. Of course, I've never been to Chicago where they say pizza is the main dish."

I couldn't stop myself from spewing words out of my mouth. They kept coming and coming, and I wasn't even sure he was paying attention to me at all. He was staring out the window, clutching the steering wheel so tightly, his knuckles were white. Meanwhile, I was in the passenger seat blabbering on like an idiot. I was nervous, and when I got nervous, I became a Chatty Kathy. My mother always told me it was one of those features I needed to work on. How could I not be nervous, though? Blake was even more gorgeous than I remembered.

When he was young, I'd thought he was hotter than hell with that perfectly charming smile, those big, firm muscles, and the way his hair was always styled just right. I remembered watching him walk along with his hand pressed on the perfect spot on his wife's lower back, showing affection but also partnership. Even at fifteen years old, that made my heart pitter-patter in my chest. But now, years later, I had to say he was even more gorgeous than when he was younger.

I glanced to the side, watching him as he drove along, my eyes wandering over the bulging muscle of his arm under his perfectly pressed dress shirt. I followed it up to his firm chin and up the side of his head. He had a bit of grey peppered on his temple and very fine lines around the edges of his eyes. They didn't make him looked old at all. What they did was make him look absolutely freaking delicious. I snapped my head back straight ahead and bit my bottom lip. What the hell was I doing? I hadn't even been there an hour, and I was already ogling my boss like he was some sort of meat on a stick. That was a no, a definite full stop. I was there for a purpose, and it was not to seduce my brother's best friend. It was to make his life easier and my life more productive. Still, the heat of his body emanated through the car, and I felt like I was having hot flashes just being close to him.

I couldn't remember the last time a man had that kind of effect on me, and in fact, I was pretty sure no man had ever done that. I'd dated a bit in high school and after, but I had so many aspirations that I tried to stay focused on my goals of working and getting through my college courses. Until now, right there in his car, my lust had pretty much stayed in my imagination and hadn't stepped out into the sun in a long time. I lived with my parents. What was I going to do? Start something with a guy and sneak him in through my bedroom window? My parents still noticed when I came in late, and I was pretty sure they would have noticed if I didn't come home at all.

My feelings had to stay hidden away. I couldn't let my childhood crush turn into anything more than that, not that I thought he was interested whatsoever. Still, I was a woman, a not too shabby looking one, staying at this rich widower's house in Boston. It sounded like the makings of a romance novel, but I couldn't let it turn into one. After packing all my things back at home and thinking about the future, I'd realized how important this job was to me. It was going to afford me the ability to make money, get out of my parents' place, and get through college like I'd been trying to do for a couple years. On top of that, he was my older brother's best friend, not someone I could hide having a relationship with. The last thing I wanted was to end up dragging my ass, tail tucked between my legs, back to California. I would be completely disgraced.

If something like that happened, I didn't even know how I would possibly explain it to my mother. She would have an aneurysm and then proceed to lecture me for the rest of my life on making smart choices. I loved my mother and leaned on her a lot. The last thing I wanted was for her to be disappointed in me.

I looked out my window as the SUV started to slow down a bit. We'd turned into a small neighborhood right outside of the city. The houses were huge, landscaped perfectly, and had that East Coast appeal to them like I imagined in my head. We took a couple of turns and pulled up to a gate. Blake typed in a code, and the big metal gates clanked as they slowly opened up, revealing a three-story house that was bigger than my high school. It was a beautiful house and bigger than anything I'd ever been inside before. He pulled into the garage and turn off the ignition before looking over at me and smiling.

"Here we are," he said. "Your home for however long you decide to stay with us."

"It's beautiful," I said, taking his lead and getting out of the car.

We went around back, grabbed my bags, and headed inside. Everything was immaculate, with granite countertops in the kitchen, hardwood floors, and stainless-steel appliances everywhere. We walked quickly through the house to the main stairwell and up to the right.

"I wanted to let you get settled in first," he said. "Before I show you the rest of the house."

He opened the door to the bedroom, and my mouth dropped open. The thing was two, maybe three times bigger than the room I had at home. Everything was beautiful, the mahogany furniture, the four-poster bed, and the light-yellow down comforter on the mattress. It made me want to lay down right there and take a nap.

"Here are the keys to the SUV," he said. "That way if you have to pick up Cooper or go somewhere, you have your own transportation. Usually, I either have a driver for work or take the Mercedes."

"Those are words I will probably never say," I laughed.

He chuckled. "I never thought about it that way. "Anyway, this is your room. Feel free to do whatever you'd like with it. It's your space. It has an attached bath, so you won't have to share with us. If you come back out of the bedroom and turn right, Cooper's room is two doors down and then my room is across from his. Feel free to explore everything whenever you'd like."

"Thank you," I said, still shocked.

"Well, I guess I'll leave you to it then," he said. "If you need anything, I'll be downstairs in my home office finishing up a few things for work for the day. Help yourself to anything we have. This is your house, too, now."

"I appreciate that."

Blake gave me a stiff nod before leaving the room and pulling the door closed behind him.

I waited until I heard his footsteps disappear down the hall before doing my own little victory dance. I stopped and laughed at myself, looking around the room. To the right, a small sitting area stretched under the window, and to the left was a large fireplace with wood already stacked inside. It seriously felt like I was in some kind of movie, like I was Cinderella or something. I wasn't sure if that made Blake Prince Charming or not, but I could make do living in the lap of luxury while I stayed here. I hadn't even thought about my living quarters until he showed me to them, but they were more than anything I would have ever imagined.

Now, all I had to do was actually start earning both the paycheck and the amazing digs. I smiled and unpacked my clothes, hanging up everything neatly and pulling out the few personal items I'd brought besides toiletries. I put the picture of my family on the dresser and stacked my books on the other end, smiling at my favorites. Between school and work, I didn't have a lot of free time, but I couldn't leave the books behind. When I was done, I wandered out and downstairs into the living room where Blake was putting on his shoes.

"I'm going to pick up Cooper," he said. "Make yourself at home."

"Thanks," I smiled. "See you when you get back."

He nodded and walked out of the house, taking the keys with him. When he was gone, I figured it was time to get acquainted with the kitchen. I was taking care of two men, and they would require food, no doubt like I remembered my brothers eating when I was younger. I went through the cabinets, opening each one, each time my arched eyebrow growing higher and higher. It was obvious grocery shopping hadn't been a priority for Blake as there was pretty much nothing in the kitchen but some old canned vegetables and frozen food.

I laughed as I grabbed a piece of paper and pen and sat down at the table to make a list. Cooking was one of my favorite things to do; something I did almost every night for my parents. It relaxed me and, at the same time, rewarded me with full bellies and happy smiles when we were done. Besides, it was just one more thing I could do to help earn my keep there since he'd negotiated an absolutely ridiculous salary for me. It looked like they could both use a home-cooked meal anyway. The stack of pizza boxes was more than any college dorm room would have.

It suddenly dawned on me that Blake needed as much nurturing as Cooper did. There was no warmth felt in the big house, making it feel more like an imposing structure than a home. I was determined to help put some of that warmth back inside its walls.

While I could never take the place of Blake's late wife, I could infuse some of my own care into these two lost souls.

And a warm, homecooked meal was a great place to start.

Chapter 5

Blake

The alarm started to beep above my head, and I reached up, hitting it with my palm. I rolled over onto my back and stretched, pulling my arms above my head and yawned. I could hear the television out in the living room and knew Cooper was already awake. The kid didn't know what the meaning of sleeping in on weekends was. It was also Aly's first real day in the house, and I had to admit, I could feel her there. It was a force, something I couldn't explain, not bad, just different. Having a woman in the house again, and a really sexy woman at that, was turning out to be more distracting than anything. Of course, it was only her first day, so I tried not to jump to any conclusions. My mind wasn't even clear enough to think about those things this early in the morning.

When Cooper and I had gotten back from school the evening before, he had met Aly for the first time. At first, he was a bit standoffish, but as we ate, she talked to him about school, about his interests, his friends, and tried to find common ground with him. She was good at communicating with him, which was more than I could say for myself. Communication between him and me was usually a head nod or a slap on the back, not a full-on conversation. Aly and Cooper though, had hit it off, getting along amazingly well. I had to admit there was a part of me that was jealous of that fact. I was a big reason why we didn't get along like that, but still, I missed his smile and his laugh.

Aly was already doing awesome things with Cooper and had plans for the household on how to make things a bit more normal on a daily basis. When we were done with dinner, I helped bring the dishes into the kitchen. Aly was at the sink rinsing and putting them in the dishwasher and called to me before I could completely walk away. She joked about the lack of food in the kitchen and expressly asked that I take her to the grocery store the next day. She was excited to use the kitchen, and she wanted to start cooking breakfast and dinner every day if she could. She said besides the benefit of proper nutrition, it would give us all the chance to sit and let Cooper talk about his day. It was surprising how much she thought about the deeper things, the things I struggled to comprehend when I thought of being a single father.

Aly was right. Cooper needed to have the opportunity to talk about his days, his feelings, the things he was going through and have me there to listen to what he had to say. Dinner was a good place to start that. So I promised to take her shopping, and it was one of the first things I planned on doing today if I could get my tired ass out of bed. I hadn't slept well at all since my wife died, and I was stuck in a perpetual exhaustion, struggling to get out of bed every day. Everyone else called it depression. I just called it life.

I sighed and dragged myself out of the bed. I shuffled across the floor to the dresser and pulled out some clothes, glancing up at my semi-grizzly appearance in the mirror. I needed to shave. My five o'clock shadow had become more like a hunter's beard, and my hair was all over the place. Normally, I wouldn't care about things like that, but I figured I'd try not to scare Aly on her first day there. I wasn't awake, though, so I made do with a comb and figured my face could wait for later. When I walked out of the bedroom and downstairs, the ever-familiar background songs of the Xbox One came from the living room. I yawned and walked into the room, stopping in the doorway to stare at Aly and Cooper on the couch, very engrossed in a video game. I had no idea how they did it that early. I had a hard enough time walking from one room to another, much less trying to coordinate my fingers and eyes for the games.

They ended the level and threw their arms up in the air in celebration. Aly high-fived Cooper, and he smiled for the first time in a very long time. His eyes shifted from her to me, and I nodded my head at him. His smile faded a bit, which made me a little sad, but at least it wasn't a frown like I usually got.

"Hey, Dad," he said.

"Oh," Aly said, standing up quickly. "I'm sorry, we were waiting for you to wake up. I figured since it was Saturday morning and all of Cooper's homework got done last night, it would be fine for him to play some games."

"It's fine," I said, waving her off. "Cooper is allowed to play video games in the morning as long as he's ready to go wherever he's going that day."

Before I could even get the whole sentence out of my mouth, Aly was already putting away the controllers and walking toward the kitchen. She looked nervous, which was something I wasn't used to. I really had forgotten what it was like to have a woman around all the time, and one I barely knew at all. It was pretty frustrating that she was so tentative about everything.

"I'll see what we have for breakfast," she said, walking toward the doorway. "I should have had it already done. I'm sorry."

"Stop," I snapped. "I'm capable of feeding myself if I'm hungry."

She stopped and put her hands down in front of her, nodding her head and pulling back. Immediately, I felt like an asshole for snapping at the girl. All she was trying to do was make sure we were fed and ready for the day, and there I was, biting her damn head off. I needed coffee, that was my problem.

I tilted my head and looked at the floor, embarrassed that I'd treated her that way. I knew I should apologize, but I wanted to sound sincere, not irritated. She faked a smile and walked back over to the couch, sitting down and giving Cooper a genuine smile as she took the controllers back out and handed one to him. I sighed and walked toward the kitchen, stopping at the door and listening.

"He just needs coffee," Cooper whispered. "He's always been like that. He's kind of a jerk in the mornings."

Aly smiled and ruffled his hair, glancing back at me before continuing with the game. I turned and walked into the kitchen, grabbing the coffee pot and filling it with water. I poured the water into the back of the machine, thinking about the fact that I owned a huge company and still used the same coffee pot my wife and I had bought when we married. It was the first time I'd ever noticed that. I started the machine and leaned against the counter, closing my eyes. Aly looked so pretty, dressed casually, her hair down around her shoulders, her bright eyes ready for the day. I had managed to ruin that in about three seconds with my grumpy-ass, non-morning person, bullshit.

As soon as the pot was full of dark, rich liquid gold, I filled my cup and took a sip, breathing in the smell of the beans. When I opened my eyes, I felt better almost instantly and walked back out into the living room. I walked over to where they were sitting and took a seat in one of the chairs next to the couch. I watched as they played their game, laughing and wincing their way through whatever battle was happening on the screen. I didn't want to interrupt that round, so I waited until it was finished.

"Yes," Cooper said, high-fiving Aly again. "That's the farthest I've ever gotten!"

"Teamwork," Aly sang.

"So, you need groceries, right?" I asked.

"Yes, please," she said, her voice returning to neutral. "What you have in there is not anything I can make any kind of meal out of."

"No problem," I said, leaning back in the chair. "I was thinking the three of us could grab breakfast before hitting up the grocery store."

"Can we go to Martha's Diner?" Cooper asked excitedly, turning to Aly. "They have the best pancakes ever."

I laughed. "Sure. Why don't you go get dressed? Then we'll head out."

"Okay," Cooper said happily.

I watched as he wound up the cord connected to his controller, did the same for Aly's, and put everything away before taking off for the stairs. He was a good kid, always did his chores, always cleaned up after himself, and I couldn't take the credit for that. It had been my wife who'd taught him those things.

Aly stood up and put her hands together before heading for the door. I knew I needed to say something to her after I had snapped at her. I didn't want to go the rest of the day in a completely awkward silence.

"Listen," I said, stopping her. "I'm sorry for snapping at you. I am not a morning person and never have been. Still, it's no excuse for being that way. You were just trying to be helpful."

"No problem," she said with a small smile.

"This whole situation is new, you know?" I said. "It was a good decision, don't get me wrong, but it'll take some getting used to. It's been a long time since Cooper and I had anyone in our lives, or in our house for that matter. I'll try not to take my pissy morning attitude out on you next time."

She nodded and chuckled, looking down at the ground. She was really sweet, and I couldn't help but notice how her cheeks got rosy when she got nervous.

"I'm gonna get ready," she said, turning quickly.

I waited until she was completely out of earshot before letting out a deep breath. I grumbled to myself, feeling like a complete idiot for having to apologize to her already. I needed to get my head on straight. Otherwise, having her here was going to be a really painful experience for both of us.

Chapter 6

Aly

After I got ready, trying to forget that Blake had chewed me out for trying to make breakfast, I headed downstairs and jumped into the SUV with Cooper and Blake. I stared out the window like a dog on his first car ride, trying to take in as much as I could. I had always been that curious girl, wishing I had the kind of life where I could travel and see the world. We went to the breakfast place, Martha's, and Cooper was right. The pancakes were probably the best things I'd ever had, along with their blueberry syrup, which was an obsession of mine. The conversation was good, but it was mostly between Cooper and me with Blake sitting quietly next to the window.

Afterward, we headed to Trader Joe's, a grocery store I loved but never could afford getting all the things I wanted. They had fresh foods, things that were super healthy, and everything I would need to start making the dishes I'd been wanting to make for years. I was like a kid in a candy store when I walked in, and I blushed, catching Blake chuckling at me. Cooper ran over to the apple section and looked over at me with excitement.

"These are my favorite apples," he said. "They're called Pink Lady, and some of them are the size of Dad's fist."

"Well, then, we should get some." I laughed, looking over to Blake for approval.

"Sure," he nodded, distracted. "Seriously, get anything you want. Fill us up."

Grocery shopping back home was an event usually made up of coupon cutting, strategic planning, browsing of all the sales before leaving, and creating basically a battle plan of where to get the best deals and how to stretch our budget as far as it could go. With Blake, it was different. Money didn't really matter. He was letting me buy anything I wanted. Seeing as I was going to be cooking for him and his son, I wanted to know what kinds of food that they were interested in.

I called Cooper over to me. "What is your favorite veggie?" I asked.

"Hmm, probably carrots," he said. "But I like all veggies. My mom really liked them, so I always ate whatever she made."

"Well, that's fantastic. What about you, Blake?"

"Anything but peas." He smiled.

Well, Blake was going to be no help in that venture whatsoever. I shrugged and pushed the cart on. If he didn't want to participate, he couldn't complain when I cooked dishes he might not like. Instead, I focused on Cooper who was my primary concern anyway since I was there to be his nanny, not Blake's. Cooper walked with me from aisle to aisle, pointing out the food he liked, talking about the things his mom used to make, and telling me about more of his interests. I could tell he was used to being on the go all the time with his mom, participating in a lot of different things. I wondered how much of that had stopped since she died. From the way he talked, it was probably almost all gone. That, in itself, was another loss the poor kids had suffered.

By the time we were through the checkout, I knew a ton about Cooper and still very little about Blake. In fact, the only thing I learned about Blake was that he didn't like peas. Cooper helped fill the cart with the grocery bags as his dad ran his credit card through the system. I was afraid he would be upset with the cost once it was all added up, but he didn't flinch or anything, just nodded and signed the credit card pad.

When we got back to the house, Blake's phone rang, and he nodded over at Cooper to help me get the groceries in. Cooper nodded in return, watching his dad walk into the house, talking to someone on the phone. I could tell that this behavior bothered Cooper, but there was nothing I could do at the moment but move forward and keep Blake in the loop, trying to make Cooper's quality of life a little better. We carried all the groceries inside and unpacked them, making different piles for fridge, freezer, and other. The entire island was packed full, and some of the fruits were stacked by the range. I grabbed a piece of paper and motioned for Cooper to come sit with me.

"Normally, I would create a menu for the week before grocery shopping, so I can have a list when I go," I explained. "But since I didn't know what you liked, we're going to do that backward this time. This is everything we bought, and now we have to come up with dishes for every night of the week using the ingredients we have. We'll go through it, and every time we write a recipe down, we'll put those ingredients away and see what we're left with for the next day. Sound good?"

"Yeah," he said enthusiastically. The poor kid was starved for attention if creating a meal plan was this exciting. "There's a lot of food here, so you want to use the stuff that can go bad quickly first, right?"

"You're absolutely right." I smiled. "You don't want to put a recipe with mushrooms in it all the way on the last day because they'll go bad. Also, things like cilantro and parsley have a short shelf life, so you want to use those first."

"Here you have tomatoes, garlic, peppers, and we got pasta," he said. "You could make homemade spaghetti."

"That's great," I said. "How did you know that?"

"My mom used to make it, and she would go buy the tomatoes the same day because she said they go bad so fast." He smiled, standing up and putting away the items he talked about. "You could even take part of the beef and make meatballs to go into it."

"I sure could. We just need to separate the meat and freeze the other half," I smiled.

Cooper seemed to enjoy doing the meal planning with me. He had all kinds of recipes stored up in his eight-year-old brain, and he was looking forward to using them. When given the chance to shine, the kid was more than bright. He remembered everything about cooking with his mom, and instead of pulling away from the memory, he embraced doing it all over again. I made a mental note to get him totally involved with the cooking and menu planning from there on out. When we were done and all the groceries were put away, I looked over at the office door, wondering if Blake was going to come out or leave us to our own devices for the day.

"So, what do you normally do on Saturdays?" I asked. "Do you have any plans with your friends?"

"Nah," he said. "I don't have many friends in this neighborhood, and Dad doesn't like to drive me to where my school friends live. He barely knows any of their parents."

"Right." I nodded. "Well, the sun is shining, and it's not too cold out yet. You want to go throw a baseball around in the yard?"

"Sure," he said excitedly. "I'll go grab some gloves and a ball. Meet you out back."

"You got it." I smiled.

He ran off to his room, a look of excitement in his eyes that made me smile. I walked out the back door and into the perfectly landscaped backyard. The grass was green, the birds were chirping, and it looked like a whole other world back there. The leaves were starting to fall from the trees, and the cascade of colors almost took my breath away. Growing up in San Francisco didn't award me seasons like this, but it was like I imagined it would be.

Cooper ran up to me. "Okay, I'm ready. Here's your glove and the ball."

"Awesome." I smiled, taking them from him.

We started to toss the ball back and forth to each other, and it was quickly very apparent to me that the kid had very little athletic ability. I knew Blake's company was sports based and sponsored the NFL. I wondered if Cooper's lack of athleticism was partly why he and his father didn't seem to be super bonded. There were many things that could get in the way of their relationship, but they'd been sheltered by his mother. Now that she wasn't in place to be that buffer, that connection, they might have had a hard time getting close again.

We tossed the ball back and forth for about thirty minutes. When he looked like he was losing interest, I walked over and tossed the ball back to him. He caught it and smiled, looking up at me.

"Let's go get a drink," I said.

When we got inside, Blake had finally come out of his office. I walked into the kitchen and got a couple of glasses of iced tea I had made earlier and took them to the guys. Blake smiled and took the glass, sipping it and setting it on the table.

"It's Saturday," he said. "Normally, unless I have something to do, you can be off on the weekends for the most part. I'm going to take Cooper out to the movies, so feel free to continue to get settled in."

"Thanks." I smiled, watching as he led Cooper out to the car.

I spent the rest of the afternoon getting my computer set up in my room and sifting through all my college information. I had to see where I needed to pick up, what classes I had to take or retake, and what kind of time was needed to get this degree done. Luckily for me, Blake had decided to pay six months' wages up front. The money he'd given me was more than enough to pay for my entire semester plus leave money for my living expenses. It was exciting to know I'd be able to get through another semester and not completely kill myself in the process. Plus I got to work with an awesome little boy and a man who was sexier every time I saw him.

Chapter 7

Blake

Monday morning was not at all what I had in mind for a fresh start to the week. I didn't even get to sleep until my alarm went off, which was set for a lot later than when my eyes shot open. I reached up and grabbed my phone, groaning and growling through the movements. I pulled the phone down and looked at the screen to see Inez's name on the caller ID. What in God's name did my assistant want before the sun had come up? I pressed the answer button and put it up to my ear, sighing heavily and dramatically into the phone.

"Don't sigh at me," she snipped. "If you did what I asked you to do, the things you said you would take care of, then I wouldn't have to call you before I've even had my first cup of coffee."

"Is the building burning down?" I groaned.

"Physically? No," she replied. "Metaphorically, it depends on what you consider a blaze."

"Okay, okay," I said, sitting up. "I get it, I've been absent lately."

"Absent? Try a ghost," Inez replied. "But that isn't why I'm calling. I need you to put on a suit and get your ass into the office. We have a bunch of stuff to go over. I'm stirring my coffee now, in my to-go cup, and I suggest you do the same."

"Yes, boss," I said, hanging up the phone.

I groaned and dragged myself out of bed, rubbing my eyes before pulling on a pair of sweatpants and T-shirt. When I walked out of my room, I stopped, realizing I was going to have to knock on Aly's door. I didn't know why I was so nervous to do that, but for some reason, my feet were glued to the floor. I shook my head, scolding myself for being such a child about it and walked over to her bedroom. I knocked and stepped back, putting my hands in my pockets and smiling as she answered.

"Hey," she said. "I was just getting ready to change and come out to start your coffee."

"Don't worry about that. I actually have to race in this morning," I said kindly. "I wanted to know if you would drive Cooper to school?"

"Um, sure," she said. "You'll have to leave me directions."

"I'll set the GPS for school and home before I leave." I smiled. "Thank you. You're a lifesaver."

"It's my job," she said with a laugh. "But you're most welcome."

I walked back to my room and jumped in the shower, getting ready quickly. Before I left, I programmed the GPS for Aly and smiled, thinking about how sexy she looked in her robe with tousled hair. When I was done, I pushed the thought from my mind. I had a lot to concentrate on, and I needed to follow Hollis's advice and get back on the train at work. It was important that I didn't let everything in my life fall to shit. When I got there, coffee in hand, Inez looked at me, narrowing her eyes.

"What now?" I groaned.

"You do remember that Jordan is throwing a party, right?"

"Uh, sure, yeah," I said, not really being honest.

"Yeah, okay, well you didn't RSVP, and he's more than a little pissed," Inez said.

"Oh lord," I said, rolling my eyes. "Fine. I'll call him and smooth it all over. There's no reason for him to get pissed. When's the party?"

"Wednesday night."

"Wednesday?" I asked. "Who throws a party on a Wednesday?"

"Your partner Jordan does," Inez said sarcastically.

I nodded and walked into my office, pulling out my cell phone and calling Jordan. He answered the phone like an angry twelve-year-old, and it took everything in my power not to laugh. In the end, I smoothed things over with him and agreed to come. I thought it was damn stupid he was throwing the party on a Wednesday, but I didn't tell him that. It would have caused even more of a problem.

"All right." I chuckled. "I'm sorry for the misunderstanding. I'll see you on Wednesday night."

I hung up the phone, my fake smile fading from my lips. I sighed and turned to my screen, moving the mouse and opening up my email. It was time I went through all the messages in there, and I hoped I hadn't missed anything super important. Most of them were from clients and friends asking how I was, wondering if I had gotten over the whole widower haze that I'd found myself trapped in. I wrote those people back with a copy and pasted version, just to give them something to chew on.

When I flipped over to the business account, I started to notice emails from the NFL. After reading about six of them, I realized our sponsorship was about to lapse, which was a huge marketing tool for us. Immediately, I went to work, calling the different departments and scrambling to get everything in order. I couldn't be mad at Inez about this. The task was mine to handle, and I had requested that it go through me personally. I had completely dropped the ball with it. It was kind of a wake-up call, to be honest, showing me how far I had fallen down the rabbit hole of depression. I had almost let the most important part of our business, the partnership that had pushed us to a new level, walk right out the door. It would have cost the company big time, and if I had lost that that sponsorship, I would have probably paid for it with my place on the board as well.

"Boss, I need you to—" Inez stopped halfway into the office and lifting her eyebrows. "Oh, you're working."

"What do you need me to do?" I asked.

"Oh, nothing I can't take care of later," she said with a smile. "I'll get more coffee for you."

"Thanks," I said, putting the papers together. "And can you mail this off same day to the NFL offices? It is our re-up for the sponsorship."

"Of course," she said, walking over and taking the large manila envelope. "Anything else?"

"No, thank you."

She walked out of the office with a smirk on her face, surprised to see me putting in real work. I didn't blame her. It had been a year of her staring at me as I stared off into space, and now all of a sudden, I was back in the game. I needed a breath of fresh air, and I wasn't sure if it was Hollis or Aly who gave it to me, but it was enough for me to realize I needed to do something. Maybe it would stick, maybe it wouldn't, but no matter what, today was going to be productive. When I was done marking down all the appropriate notations for the sponsorship in the files, I filed them away.

"Here you are, boss." Inez breezed in with a fresh cup of coffee.

"What coffee shop is this?" I asked, staring at the label.

"The one in your lobby," she said, raising an eyebrow. "You signed off on it last year."

"I did?" I looked at her like she was crazy. How could I forget allowing a coffee shop in the lobby I passed through every day?

"Yeah, and you said you would love for the coffee to be closer."

"Well, I do." I laughed. "Apparently, I've been living in a bubble the last year."

"More like a basement away from the world," she replied. "But don't let me interrupt. Keep going. You're on a roll today. You might actually get through those emails."

"On my list for next," I said as she walked out the door.

"Look at you." She laughed, closing my door behind her.

It was funny that she was more than surprised to find me actually doing something with my time in the office instead of just sitting there. I turned back to the emails and started to clean out the inbox, one email at a time. It would be nice to come back to the office the next day with a fresh start, everything taken care of, the sponsorship in the right hands, and everything ready to get rolling. When I was done with the emails, I went through my voice mails and messages from Inez from the prior week. There were several personal calls I would take later, but as for work clients, I picked up the phone and got straight back to them.

There were quite a few who were worried about the sponsorship, but I made sure they knew everything was on the right track. It felt good to have that confidence back from people again, though I assumed none of them had lost it. It had been in my own head. When I was done with the most recent missed calls, I started on the list of people I had been putting off for the last year. It was a shame I'd let myself get that far behind, but now it could all be a new beginning. Aly was going to provide a perfect amount of time for me to focus on work, but when I had gotten all caught up, I wanted to make it a point to spend more time with Cooper. He was the one who was really suffering through the whole situation.

Seeing him with Aly, laughing, playing video games, tossing a baseball, and helping with the cooking brought back old memories, and though they were painful, they were good ones. Aly fit in perfectly with Cooper, and despite having to behave myself, I kept getting a comforting feeling whenever I saw them together. She would never be able to replace my wife, but she was a needed influence in Cooper's life.

Speaking of Cooper, I looked down at the time and thought about all the work I needed to finish before I could start the next day fresh and ready. It was an absurd amount, and I could use a long night in the office. I shrugged and picked up the phone, figuring it wouldn't hurt to ask. I found Aly's number and called her up.

"Hello?" she answered.

"Hey, it's Blake," I replied. "You busy?"

"No," she said. "I was finishing up preparing Cooper's snack for when he gets home from school."

"Awesome. Listen, I'd like to have the time to get caught up on stuff at work. I was wondering if you could pick him up from school?"

"Sure," she said cheerfully. "Should we expect you for dinner or just prepare the table for the two of us?"

"Go ahead and do just the two of you," I replied. "I might be really late tonight. If you have leftovers, I'll grab them when I get home, and if not, no big deal either."

"Okay," she said. "Sounds good."

"If you have any questions feel free to call me," I said. "This is great. I got really behind at work, and this will make my life a lot easier."

"Of course," she said. "It's part of my job. Do you mind if Cooper watches a movie before bed?"

"No, that will be great. He'll like that," I replied with a smile. "And thank you so much for that."

"No need for thanks," she said. "I'll see you when you get home later."

I worked late into the night that night, Aly on my mind, my deceased wife on my mind, and the silence of the empty office around me. It felt good to be doing what was expected of me again, and I owed some of the thanks to Aly.

Chapter 8

Aly

I had gone to bed about two hours after I put Cooper down to rest for the night. We both knew Blake was going to be late, so we watched a movie, had some ice cream, and then Cooper went to sleep. I tried to stay up to get ahead some more in class, but the exhaustion from the day started to build. I lay down on my bed and closed my eyes, quickly drifting off to sleep. I wasn't sure how long I was asleep before I heard the noise, but it woke me, forcing me to sit straight up in bed. I looked over at the clock. It was almost two in the morning.

Carefully, I slipped out of bed and onto the floor, creeping over to the door and listening for a moment. I thought I could hear someone, but I wasn't positive. There were no sounds in the rest of the house. I had to be the only one who had woken up. Slowly, I exited the room and crept down the stairs. It was dark in the house, and there was no sign of Cooper, so whatever I heard came from something or someone else. I rounded the corner in the kitchen and grabbed a frying pan. As soon as I took a step forward, the light came on, and I screamed. Blake jumped and then stood frozen in the doorway, his hands up in the air and a confused look on his face.

I grabbed my chest and shook my head, trying to catch my breath. Laughing through my heavy breathing, I shook the frying pan at him. I felt completely foolish, especially since he'd told me he wouldn't be home until really late. I looked back up, and he hadn't moved a muscle, just continued to stare at me, almost awkwardly. I smiled and tilted my head trying to figure out why he was so silent. Slowly, I followed his eyes down and realized that all I had on was a very loose tank top and my blue bikini cut panties. Not only that but the shirt had shifted in my pathetic attempt to shield myself with a frying pan, and half of my breast was hanging out for the world to see.

My cheeks grew red while embarrassment flooding through my veins. I tried not to make a big deal about it. Instead, I lowered the frying pan, setting it on the counter, fixed my tank top, and crossed my arms in front of me. I looked back up at Blake as his eyes shifted up to mine, and his mouth quickly closed. I bit my bottom lip and forced my eyebrows together in irritation.

"You should let someone know when you're coming in that late," I grumbled. "You scared me to death. If I had been any closer, I might have hit you in the face with that damn pan, and then where would we be? You'd have a broken face, and you'd have to explain to everyone how you got it."

I huffed and puffed, putting my arms down and stomping past him. I didn't stop when I left the kitchen, either. I just kept going up the stairs and to my bedroom. Once I was in there, I closed the door and leaned up against it, covering my face and erupting into a quiet giggle. I couldn't believe what happened down there. I went running through the house like a superhero to find my boss standing there staring at my boobs. The man acted like he'd never seen a pair before. I laughed again and shook my head, leaning back against the door. Once the adrenaline died down, I had the good sense to be mortified.

I groaned and walked over to the bed, falling face-first into it. It was so inappropriate what had happened. For god's sake, it could have been Cooper down there. I didn't even think about it before I went hustling down to the kitchen armed with metal pans and pretty much no clothes. I hoped he wouldn't fire me over it. I needed this job, really cared about what I was doing, and was already making headway with school. I turned over onto my back and stared up at the ceiling, mortified. Blake's face blew through my mind, and without warning, a tiny smirk crossed my lips. Beyond it being horrifying, it was kind of sexy how blatantly he had gawked at my body. I couldn't help feeling slightly turned on by his more than obvious desire for me.

He was much older than me, but that made it all the more hotter, didn't it? He had the kind of experience I was pretty sure would melt me to the bed. The kind of pleasure that man could bring was more than I wanted to think about at that moment. I had to stop the thoughts and go to bed. They were as inappropriate as my parade through the house. I sighed and pulled the covers over me, falling asleep to the images of Blake's sexy body floating through my brain.

When I woke up in the morning, I made it a point to make sure I was fully dressed, socks, shoes, and all before I even thought of leaving the bedroom. I even put on a shirt that left no possibility of seeing any kind of cleavage when I bent over. I was pretty sure if I could have put on a nun's getup, I would have at that point. When I was completely satisfied I had covered any and every portion of skin that could be deemed inappropriate, I headed downstairs and started breakfast for Cooper.

He got up and got ready usually on his own and would meet me downstairs at the breakfast table, or at least that was what had happened the day before. By the time I was done making waffles and eggs, Cooper was patiently waiting at the table. We ate breakfast together, talking about his upcoming day and waiting for his dad. When Blake didn't show, and it was time for Cooper to get to school, I wrote him a note and headed out to drop Cooper off. I figured he had a late night, but surely, he would be up by the time I got back. However, that wasn't the case.

I walked into the house and hung the keys up, taking off my shoes at the door. In the kitchen, I checked to see if coffee was being made, but it wasn't. I sighed, slightly irritated that he wasn't up yet. He had responsibilities, and the first and foremost was to be a father. It wasn't right that he sleep all day, so I made a pot of coffee and headed upstairs to wake him. When I reached the top of the stairs, I almost changed my mind, feeling slightly awkward going to his room, especially after what happened the night before. Still, he needed to go to work, so I was going to suck it up and handle it. When I got to his bedroom, his door was slightly cracked. I carefully pulled it open and walked in, stopping dead in my tracks. Blake stood in front of me slightly turned away, in the middle of pulling up his pants.

Heat blew through me, my heart pounding in my chest. Blake had just gotten out of the shower, the steam still rolling off his skin. Droplets of water clung to his tight, strong body and glistened in the dim lighting of his room. His towel puddled around his feet, his muscles tightening and relaxing in front of me. His skin was tan, and the dimples in his cheeks were deep and strong, increased against his muscles. I bit my bottom lip and stared, unable to move or make a sound. He was sexy as hell, and all I wanted to do was walk up behind him and run my hands over his body.

Just then, the sound of the alarm from the coffee maker caught my ear, pulling me from my stare. I shook my head and let out a small squeaking sound as he stood up straight and turned around. I covered my mouth and squeaked again, this time spinning and running from the room. I could feel the heat in my cheeks, but embarrassment wasn't what was painting them red. Pure lust had taken me over, and I had to get away as fast as I could before I did something I would later regret.

I went straight down the stairs and into the kitchen, popping some toast in the toaster and wandering around, trying to keep my nerves intact. I reached up and grabbed a plate, fumbling with the dish when I heard footsteps approaching from behind. I didn't even want to look at him much less talk to him, but there I was and there he was, with no child as a buffer between us. I was scared that if I looked at him, all I would see was him naked. In fact, part of me fantasized that he was naked when I turned around.

"I'm sorry about that," he said from behind me. "I'm not used to someone else being in the house, and I should have locked my door. It's been a bit of a struggle for me to get used to this."

"It's only been a couple of days," I said, turning around with a smile on my face. "Besides, it was a boob for a butt. I think we're even now."

Just like me to make a joke about something so horrifically embarrassing. Sometimes, I wondered what the hell was wrong with me, but at the same time, most things seemed to be easily fixed by a little humor. I waited for his response and slowly let out the air trapped in my lungs when he started to laugh.

"I'm going to be working from my home office today." Still chuckling, he grabbed a banana. "If you need me, I'll be in there. I'll try to keep my pants on."

"Thanks," I said, blushing. He tossed the banana up in the air and walked out.

I shook my head and went back to buttering my toast. My mind wasn't on food at all. Instead, it was on that absolutely perfect ass. It was honestly the hottest body I'd ever seen. Being older than me, I knew what he could do to my body if given the chance. Untold pleasures, orgasms like no other, and just the idea of his mouth searching my body made me wet. It was becoming more and more difficult to get him out of my mind. I was drawn to him.

I sat down at the kitchen table and stared into space while I replayed the view of his body in slow motion. His level of sexiness should have been outlawed, and it was more tempting and distracting than with anyone I'd ever dated. I wanted so badly to overstep that boundary, to walk right up to him and press my lips to his, but I knew I couldn't.

This job was important and whether he fired me for that or not, it would complicate things to a point that would end my time in Boston. I had to behave.

Chapter 9

Blake

I had done everything I could to avoid Aly since the morning she'd walked in on me. It was mortifying, to say the least, and more so after the whole situation with catching her barely clothed holding a frying pan in the kitchen. The universe was trying to tempt me, a test to see how strong my willpower was, and I was failing a little more every day. I made sure my door stayed locked from the time I went to bed to the time I was fully clothed, even though I was pretty sure she would never walk in unannounced ever again.

At the same time, there was a part of me that hoped she'd done it on purpose, that she had me on the mind as much as I did her. It was distracting, sure, but I wouldn't mind if she maybe ended up naked in my bed the next time. The things I would do to a sexy little thing like her might ruin her for all other men. It had been a long time since I'd been with anyone, and the pressure and anxiety from it all were building up tighter and tighter in my chest.

As much as I enjoyed those thoughts, though, I had to push them out of my mind. Aly was fifteen years younger than me. That was a really big age difference, and I couldn't imagine we would have much in common outside of the bedroom. She was Cooper's nanny, and having something strictly sexual with the nanny, though it sounded extremely hot, would not turn out good for any of us. I didn't see Aly as the seductive type, the type of girl who would reel me into bed and be satisfied with one night of pleasure. I was pretty sure if we slept together, she wouldn't be able to look me in the eye after that. It would be the downfall of the whole thing and right after she'd gotten here.

On top of all that, if that wasn't enough, she was my best friend's baby sister, and he'd entrusted her care to me. By care, he didn't mean for me to rip her clothes off and fulfill her sexual fantasies, that was for damn sure. If anything happened between us, he would fucking kill me. There was no question in my mind. If she were hurt emotionally in the process, I could kiss my lifelong friendship with Hollis goodbye. He'd been like a brother to me for years, and I wouldn't give that back for anything in the world, not even mind-blowing sex with a twenty-three-year-old.

That was exactly what I had to tell myself every single time I started to think screwing her was a good idea. I had to look at her and see Hollis, not the sexy woman standing in front of me. I had to remind myself of everything I could lose by making one bad decision when it came to sleeping with Aly. But it wasn't as easy as it sounded. There was something about her that turned me on like no other woman before. Maybe it was the dry spell I was in, or maybe it was the fact that she was non-threatening, caring, and strikingly hot, but either way, not thinking about having my way with her was extremely difficult.

I walked over to the dresser, freshly out of the shower, pulled open the drawer, and grabbed a pair of boxers. What had she been thinking when she walked in on me naked? Because I knew exactly what I was thinking when I saw her in the kitchen. I wanted to grab her up, bend her over the counter, and fuck her until she screamed my name. I wanted to give her something special for protecting the house, and I wanted to slide those little blue panties right off her there on the kitchen floor. Her tits were so firm, so perfect, and I could already imagine what it would be like to have them in my mouth.

I pulled up my boxers and situated my hard cock. I couldn't keep doing this to myself or I was going to explode. I drew my tux from the closet, something I hadn't put on in over a year. I used to go to parties like the one I was getting ready for all the time with my wife on my arm. This would be the first one I went to all alone, and I wasn't looking forward to it in the least. I'd never been a social person to begin with, and the other parties I survived only because my wife was a social butterfly. But as I donned my tuxedo, buttoning up the pressed shirt and staring at myself in the mirror, I knew I had to fake my way through it.

After I was dressed, I headed downstairs to say good night to Aly and Cooper. They were both sitting at the dining room table, going over Cooper's math homework for the night. Math had never been his strong suit, and Aly had picked up on that fast. At least he wasn't fighting her on it, and when I got downstairs, he even had a smile on his face.

"Hey, Dad," he said. "Guess what?"

"What's that, buddy?" I asked.

"I got an A on my last math test," he said proudly.

"What?" I smiled. "That is so awesome, dude. Good job. I'm really proud of you."

"Aly taught me everything," he said, smiling over at her.

"I gave you the secrets. You did the rest all on your own." She chuckled, looking up at me.

"You look nice," Cooper said. "Where you going?"

"Oh, I have a party to go to." I sighed. "Hopefully, I won't be too late."

"Have fun." Aly smiled.

"You guys have a good night." I grinned, walking toward the door.

I jumped into the Mercedes, wishing I could go back in there and spend the evening with them instead of the people I was about to be surrounded by. The ones at the party were not the people I wanted in my life, but I had to deal with it for the company. When I arrived, I pulled my car around to the front of the mansion and handed the valet my keys. The house was twice as big as mine, and I didn't have a small place. There were tons of people already there, milling around, drinks in their hands. I walked inside and grabbed a whiskey at the bar, looking around the room. I did not want to be there. I wanted to beat home, tucked into my warm comfy bed with an old movie playing on the television.

"Blake," Joe Long, an investor for the company, said as he approached. "It's good to see you here. We've missed you at the shindigs. How are you and your son doing?"

"We're okay." I smiled. "Just taking it one day at a time. I figured this was the perfect time to start coming back out with the re-up on the NFL sponsorship and everything."

"Absolutely," he said, his attention drawn across the room. "Well, it was good seeing you. Let's grab lunch one day."

"Will do," I said with another fake smile.

That seemed to be the name of the game, fake smiles all around. It wasn't horrible talking to someone like Joe, but I still didn't want to be there. I finished my whiskey and walked up to the bar, ordering another round. A tall blonde woman walked up next to me and waited for the bartender. I could feel her staring at me, but I didn't want to turn to her.

"Can I buy you a drink?" she asked.

"Oh." I chuckled, holding mine in the air. "Got one but maybe next time."

I grinned and walked away, knowing where she was trying to lead. I walked over to the buffet and perused the different dishes. I was hungry but not really feeling like eating anything. I wanted whatever Aly was making for dinner. It had smelled amazing. I turned the corner and came face-to-face with a redhead I'd known for about a decade. I had never been close to her, and my wife despised the idea since the woman was known to be loose with her morals and her legs.

"Blake." Her smile was as fake as everyone else's. "You look amazing."

"Thank you, Emma," I said.

"If I'd known you were coming, we could have come together. How are you doing, dear? It must be lonely up there in that house all by your lonesome."

"I like the quiet," I said, scanning the room for anyone I could excuse myself for, even if it was the janitor.

"Well, if you ever want some company, you should call me up," she said with a twinkle of mischief in her eye.

"I'll do that," I said. "If you'll excuse me."

"Of course, you're an important man," she said, stepping to the side.

I greeted one of the junior partners of the company, making sure to stand there long enough for Emma to disappear to her next victim. When she was gone, I excused myself again, but this time, I made a beeline for the valet. I figured it was time to leave, even if it was early in the night. I had hit up every person I needed to talk to, and if things went the way they usually did, no one would even notice I'd left. The alcohol would begin to take control very soon, and none of them would give two shits if I was there or not. I didn't have it in me to put up with the people who wanted to talk to me. None of them cared when I wasn't around, so why did they pretend to care so much now?

When I got home, it was late enough for Cooper to already be in bed, but light came from the dining area. I shuffled through the space, undoing my bow tie and pulling it off. Aly was sitting in there, staring at me and eating something. I wanted to stop, but I didn't. I kept walking until I reached the stairs and made it up to my bedroom. She wasn't the girl for me, no matter how much she made me want to feel again. She was too young, too fragile, and my best friend's sister. I had to keep my head on straight even through the moments when her sexy blue eyes burned a hole in me.

There was a flicker of something burning inside me all the time at that point, something I hadn't felt before, or at least not in a very long time. I wanted Aly. There was no question about that. How much longer could I hold out? One more nip slip or walk-in and I might lose my ability to hold back. If she didn't seem interested, that would be one thing, but her wanting glances had me all tied up in knots.

Chapter 10

Aly

It was Friday, and Blake was at work and Cooper at school. The house was so quiet, it was almost eerie, and I couldn't stop pacing the floor back and forth. I had schoolwork to do, but I was anxious, my mind flying all over the past week. It was not what I imagined my first week working for Blake would be like. Finally, after about a hundred rotations in my bedroom, I pulled out my phone and called my sister, Tracy. I needed to talk to family before I drove myself nuts.

"Hey, little sis," she said.

"Aly," Macy yelled in the background. "We miss you."

"You're both there?" I laughed.

"Yeah, just hanging out, starting our weekend early," Tracy said. "We both took off early today, went and checked in on Mom and Dad since we don't have you there anymore, and they're doing fine."

"Are you sure?" I asked. "Because fine doesn't always mean fine."

"Believe or not, little sis, they were capable humans before us kids came around." Macy laughed.

"I know." I sighed. "I worry about them. They're always so busy and stressed, and they relied on me to get things done."

"No, they kept you busy so you wouldn't feel bad for living there," Tracy replied. "They know how you are."

"So," Macy said excitedly. "How is Boston? How's this kid you have to watch? Is Blake as good-looking as he used to be?"

"You guys are a mess." I laughed. "And yes, he's as good-looking, if not better than before."

"I knew it," Macy sighed. "He's such a stud."

"You should totally seduce him," Tracy said. "You should, like, put the kid to bed, make some drinks, put on a sexy negligee …"

"That I don't have," I said.

"Some fuzzy kitten heels," Tracy went on. "And throw some Sinatra on the record player."

"What year do you think this is?" I laughed. "You watch too many movies."

"I know, but I have to get my kicks somewhere," Tracy replied with a sigh.

"As black and white romantic as that seems," I said. "I am not going to seduce my boss. I want to keep this job. It pays well and affords me the time to get my schoolwork done. I want to graduate from college sometime this century."

"Oh, I know," Tracy said. "But it's just so hot."

"Yeah, it's like one of those porn movies where the older, hot dad seduces the babysitter," Macy said.

"Since when do you watch porn?" I laughed.

"I don't, but hell, even that sounds hot to me." She giggled.

"Okay, ladies, I'm hanging up now. Love you," I said, shaking my head.

"We love you," they both shouted into the phone as I hung up.

I put the phone in my lap, laughing and shaking my head. My sisters were wild, but they did have a point. He'd been so damn sexy when he walked through the room, pulling off his bow tie, his tux snug to his tight muscles. God, it was like fucking James Bond sauntered by me, giving me this stare like he wanted to take me right there on the kitchen table. It was insane on so many levels, unlike anything I'd been around before. But no, I could not indulge in those fantasies. It wasn't healthy and was very abnormal of me. I was not some sex-crazed woman, and I was more than capable of controlling myself.

The best thing for me to do would be to keep busy in any way I could. I turned on my computer, bringing up my college courses. There was some new work posted, and I figured there was no reason to procrastinate on it. I pulled out my textbook and started the assignment, sinking my mind into US history and the Civil War. By the time I was done with that, it was early in the afternoon. Cooper still wouldn't be home for a while, so I went to the kitchen and baked some cookies for him. I liked Cooper a lot. We'd gotten along from the first evening we met.

He was a quiet kid, but once you got him going, he had a lot to say. He'd clearly been holding back for the last year, and that made me sad. He was really into books and video games, also two of my favorite things, and had been kicking butt with cooking. I wasn't sure if he liked it or he liked the time with me, but either way, he was getting pretty good at it. He even helped me make a quiche the other night, and those take some talent and a whole lot of patience.

When the cookies were done, I arranged them on a plate and set them on the counter to cool for when Cooper got home. I walked out of the kitchen and through the house, making sure there wasn't anything to clean up. I wasn't the maid, but that didn't mean I would let the house become a wreck. When I realized everything was still as it should be, just like two hours before, I sat down and clasped my hands together. I was restless as hell, and I couldn't stop thinking about Blake. I went upstairs and started the shower, figuring a hot soak would help ease the tension a bit and get my mind back in the right place.

I pulled my hair up into a bun and took off my clothes, folding them neatly in a pile on the sink. When the temperature got hot, I stepped into the water, letting out a deep sigh as the water ran down my back. The steam blew up all around me as I ran my hands up my body, the shower spraying waterfalls over my breasts. It felt so good, too good almost. Immediately, my mind went right to Blake again, and my body did more than react. My palms floated over my nipples, the pressure of arousal making them hard. As the water trickled over my stomach and down to my hot mound, my breathing increased.

I opened my eyes and turned around to face the spray, trying to remember why I was taking another shower, to begin with. However, as the steam continued to billow out over the shower door, I pictured Blake naked with that perfect ass covered in the remnants of his own hot shower. Did he think of me, too, when he showered or when he went to bed late at night in nothing but his black boxer briefs? I'd been thinking of him, and I couldn't stop, no matter how hard I tried. I wanted to run my hands over his skin, feel that smooth, perfect ass in my hands. I wanted to know what was on the other side and just what he had in his arsenal that would rock my world.

I reached over and grabbed my loofah, squirting some vanilla chai body wash in it and ran it under the hot water, lathering it up good. I stood up straight and started to wash, at first like normal, but as I closed my eyes, I could see Blake's hot body in my mind. I pushed the loofah down my stomach and opened my legs, rubbing it gently over my pulsing pussy. Imagined walking into Blake's room late at night, finding him lying across his bed, completely naked. He opened his eyes and stared up at me in nothing more than my T-shirt and panties. A smirk moved across his face, heating my insides, making me want him even more.

Slowly, Blake sat up and pushed to the edge of the bed, putting his feet on the ground and moving toward me with finesse and charisma. Every inch of his muscular body swayed, his large cock at attention from the moment he saw me standing there. I didn't move a muscle, just watched as he walked straight up to me, cupping my head in his large, manly hands and pressing his mouth passionately against mine. I whimpered into his mouth, feeling the tip of his cock pushing against the line of my panties. He reached down and grabbed the edge of my shirt, pulling it up and over my head, letting my breasts spill out, bouncing up and down. He leaned his head down and took my nipple into his mouth, sucking on it strongly, nibbling lightly with his teeth. I moaned, pulling my hand through his hair, leaning my head back, and feeling the power of his tongue whipping across my breast.

He reached down and grabbed my ass, lifting me up in the air and turning toward the bed. Gently, he laid me down, reached forward, and slid my panties off me. I wiggled beneath him, wanting him so badly, wanting everything he could give me. He smirked, pressing me back on the bed, and lying down between my legs. He smiled as he pushed his face down into my juicy pussy, immediately running his tongue through my folds. I moaned loudly, feeling the heat immediately shoot into my stomach. His tongue slid up through me and swirled around my clit, sending electric pulses through my entire body. I screamed out, reaching my hands above my head and arching my body into the air. I could feel every hair stand up on the back of my neck as the sensations moved through me.

Just when I didn't think it could get any better, he slipped two fingers inside of me, pushing them deep inside and flickering the tips. A growl pushed from my chest. Every part of me aching to have the girth of his cock deep inside of me. My orgasm simmered so near, all I wanted was to come all over him, but I had to hold back. I had to wait for that rock-hard dick. I reached down and grabbed his face, pulling it up toward mine.

"Fuck me," I whispered as he hovered over me.

"My pleasure," he growled.

He lowered his body down and pushed forward, letting his cock slide through my juices. I gasped as he pushed harder, sinking as deep inside me as he could go. I lifted my legs up to his sides while he smoothed his hand down my thigh and began to pulse in and out of me. My breathing increased with his movements until I was so out of breath, I could barely contain myself. Screams echoed through my mind as he groaned deeply into my ear. I reached up and dug my fingernails into his back, pulling him toward me with force.

"Come for me," he whispered.

"Yes," I moaned.

He moved his hips like a snake, his body rubbing against my clit as he fucked me harder and faster. I closed my eyes, burning with the heat of passion between us, the orgasm in me beginning to boil over. He grabbed my hips, swooping down and pushing as deep inside as he could, exploding every bit of control I had left. My body tensed and he arched his back, both of us writhing in passion as we came at the same time. I closed my eyes, every wave washed through my muscles until I couldn't breathe anymore.

As the orgasm subsided, I opened my eyes again, but there was no Blake, no bed, no hot crazy sex, just me and my loofah in the shower alone. I put my hand on the wall trying to stabilize myself. If he could do that in my fantasies, I couldn't even imagine what it would be like in real life.

Chapter 11

Blake

Everything had been so good with work the past several days. I'd been pushing through things, getting shit on track, and going home feeling accomplished. However, as the days crept by, I found myself starting to feel lackluster yet again. The energy of the past few days was completely gone, and I couldn't find a way to get it back. I needed to be on my game. I needed to get through the pain of that never-ending listlessness I'd been in for a year, but there I was, tapping my fingers on the desk, staring off into nowhere. I tried to hide it from Inez, but I could see the look of disappointment curled up on her face. There was no fooling her. She'd been my assistant for years and had been the one who kept everything together in the beginning. She knew when I wasn't on my game; I didn't even have to say anything. This was one of those times when she picked up on it before I even had a chance to sit down at my desk.

"Blake," Inez said over the phone's intercom. "Brandon Ives is on line one for you."

"Who?" I replied.

"One of the other sponsors," she said. "Remember? The guy with the crazy-looking hairpiece."

"Oh, yeah," I sighed. "All right, thanks."

I waited until Inez hung up the intercom and then sat for a second with my hand on the phone. I didn't feel like talking to the guy. He was like a cheesy car salesman, the kind who nobody wanted to deal with but everybody did because he was made of money.

"Brandon," I said with fake enthusiasm. "Good to hear from you."

"Blake, my man," he said. "It was so good seeing you at the party."

"You, too, buddy," I lied. "What can I do for you today?"

"Oh, man, this is kind of embarrassing. I was calling because there was this woman, Eliza, at the party who was interested in getting to know you," he said.

"Wow," I replied, grimacing. Now this douchebag was playing matchmaker? "That's interesting. I mean I appreciate it and everything, but honestly, I'm not really in a place for dating right now. I'm still not quite over losing my wife."

"Oh, I get it man," he said. "Just thought I would let you know."

I talked to him for a few more minutes to placate him, promising to call for lunch when I had no intention to actually do so. I had zero interest in him or the woman he was talking about. I had been with a beautiful woman who'd cared way too much about the money, and I wasn't about to go down that road again. I hung up the phone and sat back in my chair for a minute, exhausted from the call. I needed some air, so I stood up and walked out of my office, strolling through the different rooms down the hallways.

Photos and memorabilia from the NFL as well as other organizations we sponsored covered the walls. They had given me something every year since the company got involved. There used to be pictures of my wife, who had done work for the company in the beginning, but I'd gone through and taken all of them down. I couldn't bear to look at them anymore.

I stopped in the hallway and stared at a picture of Pittsburgh Steelers head coach Mike Tomlin and me shaking hands and smiling. It had been a big day for me. I loved the Steelers, and the NFL had set my family and me up with box seats and allowed me to go back to the locker rooms. My wife had stayed upstairs seeing to Cooper since he was so little, but I had the time of my life. I shook my head, wondering where that happy guy had gone, and headed back to my office. A smothered sensation crept over me, and I couldn't be there any longer. I gave up trying and left for home. At least there, I could get out of the suit and into some more comfortable clothing. I'd had enough of trying to be normal for one day.

I packed up my briefcase in case I decided to work from home and ignored the irritating stares I was getting from Inez. She knew it was probably the best thing for me to do. I wasn't going to get anything done sitting there in that mood. She nodded her head to me as I left, not saying a word. I had driven the Mercedes to work that day, so I jumped in and headed toward home.

When I got there, the house was quiet, and I walked through to the kitchen to see if I could find Aly anywhere. She wasn't downstairs, so I grabbed a bottle of water and headed upstairs to get changed. I figured she was in her room, working on school work or something. However, as I passed her bedroom, her door was slightly ajar, and I stopped in my tracks. I could hear the water running in her shower, but even more than that, I could hear loud moans echoing off the tiled walls. It stopped me short. I peeked into her bedroom. Her bathroom door was ajar as well. Everything in me wanted to walk in there and look inside. I wanted to see her pleasuring herself, to watch that sexy body in the hot water writhing in ecstasy, but I didn't. It was wrong, I couldn't go spying on the girl because she lived in my house.

Those sounds, though, that deep moan that pushed from her chest, were not only arousing but exciting as well. I hadn't heard a woman moan like that in a very long. My cock was rock solid in my pants, and I stepped forward toward her door just as the shower was turning off. The change of sound knocked me back to my senses, and I turned, shuffling quickly down the hallway to my own room. I walked inside and quietly shut the door behind me, not wanting her to know yet that I was there.

The idea that Aly was pleasuring herself in the shower was absolutely nuts to me. The vision of that steaming hot stream of water washing over her soft, supple skin was hot enough, but to add the vision of her fingering her sweet pussy was driving me absolutely wild. I reached down and grabbed my cock, groaning at how hard it was.

Every fiber of my being wanted more. I wanted to hear more of those moans, I wanted more time to sit there and listen to her, and I wanted to know what she was fantasizing about. Was it me? That thought alone, the fact that she might have been pleasuring herself to thoughts of me, made me want to walk back to her room, throw her on the bed, and fuck her senseless. I wanted to make it so she didn't walk right for days. I could pull her on top of me and watch those perfect tits bouncing up and down as she rode my cock into another orgasm. I bet she was really tight, really wet, and from the sounds of her moans, a hell of a lot of fun to fuck. She had the perfect number of curves, just enough hips for me to grab onto and really dig into her. I wanted so badly to be the one forcing those moans and screams from her throat. I wanted to watch her beneath me, her head back, her tits bouncing as I plowed her over and over again.

I put my hands up behind my head and puffed the air out of my chest, shaking my head. This wasn't good. I shouldn't be standing in my room thinking about fucking my son's nanny, a woman way younger than me. I rolled my neck from side to side, trying to relax my body. I walked over and picked up the most boring book I could find off the shelf and opened it up, starting to read immediately. I had to get her out of my head. I needed to will my boner away so I could continue on with my day like a normal person.

After about two chapters, my cock had softened, so I changed my clothes and pulled on a pair of shorts, everything simmering down finally. I turned and walked from the room, not even looking at Aly's door as I passed. When I got downstairs, I looked around for food for a minute and then found the plate of cookies on the counter. She must have baked them right before she got in the shower because they were still gooey and warm in the center. Just like I pictured she was.

No, stop it! I told myself, shaking my head. For Christ's sake I was like a horny teenager. I finished my cookie and chugged a bottle of water, washing it down. I could hear Aly's footsteps coming down the stairs, and I didn't want to get into a deep conversation with her. Her moans were still echoing through my mind.

I shut the fridge and headed out of the kitchen and back toward the stairs. Aly was coming around the corner as I was getting close. She stopped and looked up at me with a smile, surprised to see me. She was fully dressed, but her hair was still wet from the shower. At first, I thought about not doing anything but nodding, but as soon as I saw that face and imagined her again up there writhing in that shower, a smirk moved over my lips. She looked at me wide-eyed for a moment, and I turned, whistling as I walked up the stairs. I chuckled to myself as I went, knowing it was a cruel game to play, but I didn't want her to think I was in any way upset by walking into that. I couldn't tell her how I felt, and I couldn't act on how I felt, but that didn't mean I couldn't engage in a little innocent flirtation in the process.

Her cheeks had instantly turned red when I smirked. There was no doubt she knew that I knew what she was doing up there in the shower. Her coyness, her innocence even, it was hot as hell. The fact that she was at all embarrassed about me hearing turned me on big time. I was used to women doing anything and everything to get my attention, but I was not used to a shy girl with a body like hers. Part of me hoped the redness on her cheeks also had something to do with who she was thinking about while she brought herself to orgasm.

Maybe it was all wrong, maybe it was inappropriate, but in that moment, after struggling through work and through the day, it made everything so much better. I didn't care if it was wrong anymore. It was the most amazing greeting from work I had ever received, and I kind of hoped there would be a repeat performance. Only next time, I might not be able to keep my cock to myself.

Chapter 12

Aly

Everything was hazy and it felt like it was going in slow motion. I was in the sand, the beach close by, but I couldn't see it for the fog. Below me, his hands wrapped tightly around my waist, was Blake. My body was moving wildly, riding his big, hard cock. I bounced up and down on top of him, swirling my hips around and around. I opened my mouth to scream out in pleasure, but nothing came out, only the sound of the water rushing the beach. His hands slid up my tits and grabbed onto them tightly as he growled wildly. My thighs were starting to shake, but my body drew closer and closer to the finish line. He moved his hands back down to my waist and started to pick me up and slam me back down on his cock. I growled, the fire burning deep inside of me. Just as I was about to explode, my eyes opened wide and I found myself lying in my bed, alone.

It had been a dream, a really hot, crazy, sexy dream about my boss. Every single stroke of his hands had felt so real, so pleasurable. I wanted so badly to go back to sleep, to explode in orgasm on top of him, but that was not an option. I was incredibly turned on, my panties wet and my nipples rock solid. I rubbed my legs back and forth against the sheets, feeling the power of his presence down the hall from me. There was no way I was going to be able to get out of that bed until I had come, so I quickly pushed my hand inside my panties and closed my eyes, rubbing hard against my clit until I exploded in ecstasy. This time, however, I kept my lips firmly shut, making very sure I didn't make a single sound.

When I was done, I rolled over in the bed and groaned, now wide awake in the middle of the night. When I was home and couldn't sleep, I always baked, and that was exactly what I was going to do now. I threw on some pants and a sweatshirt and headed down to the kitchen, figuring I'd probably be the only one awake at that hour.

In the kitchen, I started to pull out ingredients, deciding that a cake would be the best thing for me to bake. I started mixing the sugar and butter together, my mind partly on my dream and partly focusing on what I was doing. In the background, I heard the door to the home gym open and close again. Blake had apparently been working out, and I had no idea he wasn't in bed yet. I glanced over my shoulder as he entered the kitchen and opened the fridge. He grabbed a bottle of water out and walked over, sitting down at the table, not saying a word. He wasn't wearing a shirt, and immediately, my mind went blank. All I could see were those rippling muscles, that tight chest, and the visions from my dreams where he was lifting me up and down on his cock. The heat between my legs began to rise, and I fanned myself.

When I'd first arrived, I'd seen glimpses of his tattoos from afar. They pretty much covered his shoulders, his biceps, and moved across his chest. From afar, they were impressive, but now that I could see them up close, I realized how beautiful they were. He had scenes from under the water, scenes from space, and words etched into the waves talking about the beauty of life. I never thought of him as someone that deep, but it was a nice change of pace. I wish I could say, though, that the tattoos were the only things I was admiring. To be honest, the chest they were covering was a work of art in itself. It was obvious he took good care of his body.

He had a home gym, but he also had a gym membership, and I was used to him leaving for the gym in shorts and a T-shirt and coming back showered and clothed. I was not used to him walking into the kitchen, half dressed, his body absolutely amazing, and his muscles glimmering under the sweat. I wanted to rub my hands all over him. My mind was racing, thinking about him sitting behind me at the table. I was so distracted, I picked up the salt instead of the sugar and nearly poured it into the cake batter.

"Damn it," I said, jumping back and spilling salt everywhere.

"You okay?" he asked from behind me.

"Yeah," I sighed, cleaning up the mess.

"So, why are you baking at one in the morning?" he asked. "I thought I was the only one who did weird things in the middle of the night."

"Whenever I couldn't sleep at my parent's house, I would go into the kitchen and bake something," I said. "My father was a huge fan of my insomnia since it meant he would wake up to something sweet and delicious waiting on the counter. I couldn't sleep for some reason. I have to keep my mind busy, or I'll drive myself crazy lying there staring up at the ceiling wishing for the sheep to count. How about you? Why are you working out at one in the morning?"

"Same," he said. "I couldn't sleep. Actually, I was having some seriously crazy dreams."

"You have no idea," I said under my breath.

"What's that?" he asked.

"Oh, just that I was having crazy dreams too." I smiled. "I kept falling asleep and waking up, falling asleep and waking up over and over again. It was frustrating."

I finished mixing the cake batter and pulled out the two pans I'd already greased. Carefully, I split the batter between the two pans and then put them into the oven. I closed the oven and wiped my hands off before sitting down across from him at the table. I was struggling to concentrate on anything other than how hot he was. I had to force myself to look into his eyes to avoid staring at his chest. The problem was that his eyes were absolutely gorgeous as well. I could totally see myself staring deeply into them while I let him ravage my body. I cleared my throat, trying to shake the thoughts, and looked up at him with a grin. I was glad he couldn't read my mind.

He leaned back in his chair, looking relaxed. For the first time since I had gotten there, he looked happy. Normally, he walked around with that grumpy grimace on his face, saying not much more than he had to. Not now, though. Right now, he looked like someone who was actually enjoying his life.

"So how's everything going with Cooper?" he asked. "You guys seem to get along great."

"You know, it was one of the things I worried most about before coming here," I replied. "But I'll be honest, it was so easy for us. I don't know why. Maybe he needed a break from the things that happened, you know, someone to break the silence."

"Yeah, I can see that," he sighed. "It's been really hard on him since his mom died. The house has been different, his routine has been different, and of course, he misses her a lot. They were close, and she stayed home to take care of him, so she was a daily, hourly, whatever, presence in his life."

I wanted to bring him up, but before I could, the bell rang, letting me know the cakes were done. I pulled them from the oven and sat them out, letting them cool for a few minutes before putting them on the cooling racks. I brought them and the big bowl of icing to the table and sat back down. I had to wait for them to cool off first. As I waited, my mind went to what Cooper and Blake had been through.

"I'm sorry you guys went through so much," I said.

"Thanks," he said, looking down. "I think right now all I want to do is move on with my life. There's no coming to terms with it. It's a messed-up situation. All we can do now is move forward and try to get our lives into working order."

"I agree," I said, glopping icing on one of the cakes. "Did you know your son is one hell of a cook?"

"Cooper?" he said, pulling his eyebrows together. "Really?"

"Yeah, man." I laughed. "He has all kind of ideas and really gets into it."

"Huh," he said. "I didn't even know he was interested in cooking."

Without thinking, it flowed from my mouth like word vomit. Normally, I was a pro at thinking before I spoke, but tonight, I didn't seem to have a filter. Cooper had been on my mind, and his relationship with his dad was less than it should have been, but that didn't necessarily mean I should have said it out loud.

"Maybe you should spend some more time with him," I said. "Get to know your son better."

As soon as I said the words, I froze, slowly looking up from the cake. Obviously, that was the wrong thing to say, and it was written all over his face. He put his bottle of water down and stood up without another word. I watched as he marched out of the room, upset. I knew I should call after him to apologize or something, but I didn't. I wasn't wrong in what I said. He needed to get to know his son, let his son know he loved him still. The whole situation was hard on everyone involved, and I was walking into the aftermath, but as the person who now spent the most time with Cooper, I could see it was becoming more and more important to get him and his father into a better position.

I finished up frosting the cake and wrote Cooper's name on it, thinking the attention would hopefully make him smile in the morning. When I was done, I cleaned up the kitchen, put the cake on the stand, and headed back up to my room. Blake's door was shut, but his light was still on, and for a moment, I considered knocking on his door. However, the fear of losing my job or getting a stern talking to changed my mind. I shrugged and sighed, figuring he would either come around or he wouldn't, but if it meant there was a chance he would become more involved in Cooper's life, then maybe it was worth it. Sometimes, the truth was hard to hear.

Chapter 13

Blake

I barely slept a wink Saturday night, tossing and turning, getting up, pacing, moving around, thinking over and over again about what Aly had said to me. She told me I didn't know my son, and it wasn't only what she'd said that had me on fire. She'd said it so matter-of-factly, she might as well have told me what we were having for dinner the next night. When the words first came out of her mouth, I was shocked. I didn't know what to say, but as they sank into my brain, I became angry. I knew walking away like that didn't solve anything, but to be honest, I didn't know what to say to that statement. If I had talked, I would have gone off on her, belittling her or making it seem like her time with my son wasn't valid.

She had come in and, in one night, changed the way my son was acting. There was no way I could be upset with that, but what was she seeing about our relationship in that short amount of time that led her to believe I didn't know Cooper? Had he said something to her, or was it so obvious in the way we interacted that someone who didn't know us at all was able to pick up on it that fast? I was starting to second-guess myself and the time I'd put in as a father.

I had tried, hadn't I? When Cooper was younger, the three of us were a really close-knit family. We did everything together and went out of our way to show Cooper what it was like to grow up in a loving family unit. However, once the business was up and running, I was working non-stop, and he spent most of his time with his mom. When she died, I'd pushed everyone away, Cooper included. I wasn't sure how to be a person anymore, much less a father. It was something I needed to work on, that was for sure, but I still didn't know how to take that criticism without getting angry. I guess it was only natural to feel that way because I loved my son.

I sat up in the bed and let out a deep breath, pulling myself upright and rubbing my eyes. I was exhausted, not only physically, but I was exhausted from thinking about everything all night. I needed to clear my head, but at the same time, I couldn't keep running away from this issue. It was like Aly told me something I already knew but didn't want to admit to myself. At the same time, though, Inez had been saying it to me forever, just not in such a direct manner. There had been several occasions when she tried to sit and talk to me, tried pulling me from the deep hole I was in, but I didn't listen.

Every time I got that low, it was hard to feel like I was even the right person to be there for Cooper. He needed an Aly a long time ago, and it seemed I needed an Aly, too, in order to make the obvious known to me. It pissed me off that this was how it was going to go down, an almost stranger letting me know I wasn't up to par at being a father. There was no way I was going to let that pass. Whether I was mad about the way it was presented or not, I was going to start trying to make things right with my son. The last year, I'd left him alone to deal with the death of his mother when we could have been facing the storm head-on, hand in hand, like a father and son should do. Fear and anger had driven me, and I found myself unable to step forward until now.

I got out of bed and threw on some clothes. There was no reason to prolong things. Time with Cooper was invaluable, and I needed to start being a part of his life before he no longer wanted me in it. I walked out of my bedroom and passed Aly's open door, noting that she wasn't inside. I ended up finding her in the kitchen, making some coffee and getting ready for yet another day. When I walked in, she jumped slightly, putting her hand to her chest.

"You scared me," she said timidly. "I didn't hear you come down the steps."

"Sorry about that," I said. "Look, I want you to go ahead and take the day off. I'm going to take Cooper out for the day."

"Yay," Cooper cheered from his seat at the table.

"All right," she said, searching my face. "You two have fun."

Cooper ran to the front door and threw on his shoes, ready to leave the house. We jumped into the SUV and headed out to breakfast so he could get some pancakes and I could drown myself in coffee. After I was done with my first cup, I looked across the table at Cooper eating.

"Are they good?" I laughed.

"Really good," he said. "Thanks for bringing me to breakfast."

"Sure." I smiled. "I was thinking we could go over to the Discovery Museum when we're done with this. They have a space event going on there today and apparently some cool IMAX movies playing."

"That sounds great," he said, getting oddly quiet.

"What is it, bud?" I asked. "We don't have to go there if there's another museum you'd like to visit. I just remember your mother telling me you liked places like that."

"I do," he said. "It's not that."

"Then what is it?" I asked.

"You don't really like stuff like that do you?" Cooper asked, hanging his head lower. "I tried to be good at sports, but I'm terrible at it. I know that's what you like to do."

I sucked in a breath as though he words were a physical slap to the face. It was time I had a serious talk with my son. "Buddy," I said, feeling about an inch tall. "You think I don't hang out with you because you don't play sports? Man, I'm so sorry, Cooper. I never wanted you to think something like that. Listen, when your mom died, it was really hard. You know that, and well, it was really hard for me too. I messed up, though, and instead of coming to you, grieving with you, I pushed a lot of things in my life to the side. I know it all doesn't make sense to you, and it shouldn't. You're only eight years old. I didn't do what I was supposed to do as a father. I didn't protect you from the hurt."

"How could you?" he asked.

"That's a good question," I said. "I couldn't have, I guess, but I could have made this whole situation a lot less traumatic if I was there to hold your hand and walk through it with you."

"I know," he said, lowering his head. "But you were so sad too."

"That isn't an excuse," I said. "I should have been there. But here's the thing. I can't go back and erase the mistakes I made. What I can do is make sure we don't lose out on any more time with each other. I can promise you I'll do my best to be a better dad to you, to be involved in your life and the things that interest you. I want to know what's going on with you, you know? I want you to feel like you can always come to me, and I think it's important as we heal from losing your mom."

"I'd like that, Dad," he said in a tone that was way beyond his years..

"Good," I said, smiling. "Now eat up. We need to get to the museum."

"Yessss!" Cooper smiled.

I watched my son as he ate and it nearly brought tears to my eyes. To think that the most precious person in the world had thought I didn't want to be around him was painful. And I had no one to blame but myself. I mentally kicked myself for what I'd done or failed to do for him over the past year and vowed to set it right.

Cooper finished his breakfast, and we headed out to Discovery. We laughed, we talked, and we had a great time being together. I missed that part of life, the part that gave me freedom to be the kind of father I knew I could be. Cooper was so smart and didn't act like any typical eight-year-old I'd ever met. I guess in some ways, he had to grow up fast and that was part of why it was so important I start stepping back into his life. I needed to eventually talk to him about how he was doing with his mother's death, but today, I wanted us to enjoy our time together.

We watched two IMAX movies together back to back before calling it a day. When we walked out of the theatre, Cooper stretched his arms over his head and smiled big. It felt good to know he was having fun with me.

"So, I have an idea," he said.

"What's that?"

"Aly's been working hard, taking care of us," he said. "I think we should take dinner home to her."

"I think you're right,' I said, putting my arm over his shoulder. "I think she deserves more than that, but let's start with dinner. What kind of takeout?"

"She loves Italian, so let's get Piper's," he said excitedly.

"Perfect," I replied.

We picked up a bunch of food from the Italian restaurant and headed back home. When we got there, Aly was in the kitchen grabbing a drink. Cooper ran straight in and hugged her tightly.

"Oh." She laughed. "You look like you had a good time."

"We did," Cooper replied excitedly. "And we brought home dinner for all of us. Italian."

"You did?" She smiled. "Well, that's awesome."

"I thought maybe we could eat and watch Harry Potter," I said with a smile.

"I like that idea," she replied, nodding at me in understanding.

We unpacked the food, fixed our plates, and headed out to the living room to watch the movie. It was Cooper's favorite, and he decided he wanted to start with the first one, and every time we had a movie night, we would move on to the next. At the beginning, we all sat around eating, staring happily at the screen. When we finished our food, I got up and took all the dishes to the kitchen. I walked back out to the living room and stopped for a minute, staring at Cooper sitting close to Aly, talking about the movie.

Everything was so comfortable, so homey and family-like. My first instinct was to go with what was familiar, but as I slowly sat down at the other end of the couch, I started to feel uncomfortable with it. It wasn't that I wasn't enjoying myself, but there was something about Aly in the picture that felt so right. In fact, it felt so right that it was suffocating me. I was terrified to have those feelings again, to feel safe and comfortable in a situation like that. It wasn't supposed to be that way with her. She was supposed to just be the nanny.

After several minutes, the heaviness of it was too much, so I carefully got up and walked around the couch, trying not to have Cooper notice. I was successful in that, but as I walked toward my office trying to catch my breath, Aly looked back at me from across the room, the deep blue of her eyes looking sad that I was leaving. I couldn't tell if that sadness was for her or for Cooper, but I wasn't ready to explain yet.

Chapter 14

Aly

It was Wednesday, three days after we'd watched Harry Potter and had a good evening together. Since then, though, Blake had turned back to his quiet, brooding self. He hadn't communicated with me very much at all. Our only conversations were Cooper related. It was like all the progress made that day had been washed away, and I had no idea why. I regretted putting my foot in my mouth about Cooper, but he was an amazing kid with a dad who didn't seem to know how to get out of his own head. Whether it affected their relationship or not, something had to be said to him. Everything seemed to be going great to that effect on Sunday until we all sat down to watch the movie together. It was comfortable and easy, and I was pretty sure that was what scared him off.

I had seen him getting up and escaping to the silence of his office, and though Cooper didn't notice, probably because it was old hat to him, I did. I noticed the look of confusion in his eyes. I felt like I was the reason he didn't finish out what seemed to be a perfect day between the two of them. He'd run off like a scared puppy, and ever since then, it had been nothing but radio silence between us.

It was driving me absolutely insane, and his stubbornness was the worst of it all. He had been almost going out of his way to work late again, not coming home until well after midnight. I had made it a point to stay up and make sure he came home every night because I wanted to make sure he was safe. On top of that, I didn't want another false intruder situation leaving me standing in the kitchen in my underwear. Cooper seemed to be slipping back into silence too, starting to notice his father's regression, but there wasn't much I could do about it. I had to be there for Cooper and wait it out, hoping Blake came back around. Today, I woke up to fix breakfast and noticed Blake was still there, shut up in his room.

I quietly cooked Cooper some eggs and toast and waited for him to come down ready for school. He wasn't much of a morning person, just like his dad. I let him fully wake up over breakfast before saying anything. It had become a routine of ours, sitting quietly across the table from each other, thoughts of his father running through both of our heads, but nothing actually being said about it. I could tell Cooper appreciated me not pushing the subject, and I didn't want to bring it up anyway, not before he left for school. He needed to be focused and ready to attack his day, not thinking about things like his father's adult issues.

"You ready for school?" I asked, putting our dishes in the sink.

"Yeah," he said quietly. "I just gotta grab my bookbag from upstairs."

"Okay." I smiled, smoothing down his hair.

I went out to the SUV and started it up, getting the heat running. It was starting to get cold in the mornings now with winter approaching. Cooper came back out to the car and smiled as he buckled his seatbelt, and we headed off. I pulled up out front of his school and handed him his lunch.

"Have a good day, okay?" I smiled. "You're already halfway through the week."

"Thanks," he replied, getting out of the car.

It made me sad watching him walk into the school, obviously with his father on his mind. The teacher waved at me and put his arm around Cooper's shoulder, leading him inside. Hopefully, he would perk up and have a good day, at least until he got home. I headed back to the house and went straight upstairs, excited to continue my classwork. I was making great headway with my work and wanted to continue that streak. As I opened the course on my laptop, though, my phone rang, and I saw Hollis's name appear on the screen. I smiled and picked it up.

"Hey there, big brother," I said.

"Hey there, little sis," he chuckled in response. "Did I catch you at a bad time?"

"No, you actually had perfect timing," I said. "I just got back from dropping Cooper off and hadn't started my schoolwork yet. What's up?"

"I wanted to call and check up on everything," he said. "See how it is going, if you're having a good time."

"It's going great," I said. "Cooper's an amazing kid, and I'm keeping up with my schoolwork. It's exactly how you wanted it to be."

"And Blake?" he asked. "Is he being good?"

"Yeah," I said in a curious tone.

"He's not being pervy or anything, right?" he asked. "Because if he is, I'll get on a plane today and come down there and kill him."

"No." I laughed. "Of course, he isn't being pervy or anything. I barely see him at all. He leaves early for work or shuts himself in the office and comes home really late."

"Good," Hollis said. "And how about school? Are you liking it?"

"I don't know if liking it is the best term." I laughed. "But it's meeting my expectations, and for the first time in my college career, I'm getting all my work done early, I'm prepared for the next lesson, and I'm getting killer grades in all of my classes."

"That's great to hear," he said.

"How about you?" I asked. "You holding down the fort for me?"

"Always." He chuckled. "Though I have to say our mother is not thrilled that her baby girl is all the way on the other side of the country and barely ever calls her. You know how she is."

"Yeah to me, but you guys could get lost in the jungle somewhere, and she wouldn't be upset you didn't call," I scoffed.

"The trials and tribulations of being the youngest child," Hollis sighed. "But I'm serious. You need to call her."

"I will," I said. "I promise. I just completely blanked this week so far. There's been a lot going on with Cooper and school, and then there's my work. I know it's not an excuse, but I promise I'll call her."

I sat on the phone for about another twenty minutes or so, talking to Hollis about his life, what was going on back at home, and how Boston was. When I hung up with him, it occurred to me I had a big, happy, very close family, and I hadn't been shown any other type of family in my life. Because of that, I didn't understand the dynamic between Blake and Cooper. Everybody had a different family dynamic. Some were close like ours, some were more businesslike, and some were like Cooper and Blake's. They stayed out of each other's way, they made do with the relationships they had, and they didn't move from that. I was sure Cooper's mother changed that dynamic quite a bit, but she was gone, and this was what they were left with. I had to remember that when I pushed things on Blake. I needed to do better with fitting my expectations to their family style and not my own.

I sighed and turned back to the computer, moving the mouse and turning the screen back on. There was nothing I could do about any of it, so it was best to focus on school and handle everything else later. The day went by quickly, and before I knew it, I was getting dinner ready and putting it in the oven before leaving to pick up Cooper from school. He was in a much better mood when I picked him up than when I'd dropped him off, and he and I had a fantastic time eating dinner together and talking about his assignments for that week. I wanted to watch a movie with him again, but he had homework that had to come first.

After dinner, he went upstairs to work, and I cleared and washed the dishes. I took him some dessert before bed and then went back up when it was bedtime. I tucked him in and smiled as he hugged me tightly. The kid had pretty much stolen my heart. When he was good and asleep, I went to my room, leaving my bedroom door open in case he called for me, and jumped in the shower really fast. When I got out, I walked into the bedroom from the bathroom with my towel wrapped around me. I stopped at the sound of footsteps coming up the hall, and before I could move again, Blake rounded the corner, catching me in nothing but the towel and wet hair.

He stopped in the doorway, and I froze, clutching the top of my towel and staring at him with wide eyes. He didn't make any kind of move, just stared at me from the doorway. We stayed like that for several awkward moments before he took a step forward. I watched as he moved through my room, stopping in front of me close enough to smell the cologne on his shirt. Slowly, he picked up his arm and ran his finger down the slope of my shoulder, sending goosebumps all over my body. My nerves flip-flopped inside my stomach at the simple touch of his hand.

I bit my bottom lip and looked up at him, catching his deep stare. I tilted my head studying his normally vibrant eyes, and that was when I caught a whiff of whiskey on his breath. He was drunk, and not just a little, I realized as I noticed the swaying motion of his body. Wherever he had gone after work, he had come home completely wasted. I only hoped that he had been smart enough to take a cab home.

I looked back up at him, and his face was still perfectly straight, no reflection of emotion on it at all. The cold temperature of his finger pressed against my hot skin, and I tried to control my breathing. He dropped his hand to his side and turned around, walking back toward the door. When he reached it, he looked back over his shoulder and let his eyes scan me from top to bottom.

"I'm sorry," he said, reaching for the door handle.

I stood frozen until he completely shut the door all the way. My shoulders relaxed, and I let out the air I was holding tightly in my lungs. I rushed forward and flipped the lock on the door, knowing it was for the best, even if I did wish in the back of my mind that he'd come crawling into my bed. My heart was pounding in my chest, and I stood there, my thighs clenched, needing him more than I ever had before.

Chapter 15

Blake

The alarm blared in my ear, making the thumping in my head a reality. I groaned, reaching up and pressing the button, the effects of all the alcohol I had drunk the night before landing on my head. I felt like complete and total dogshit, and to make matters worse, I had some weird dream of Aly, standing in a towel, and me running my finger down her arm. It felt so real, like I could almost see her in my head still, standing there, dripping wet, surprised at my forwardness.

I turned over in bed and stared up at the ceiling, thinking about the night before. The bar was packed, but I didn't know anyone there, which was exactly why I went to a bar away from the office. I hadn't really talked to anyone either. I'd been in a mood of sorts. I'd had a bad day, undoubtedly. I was in the middle of work when the weight of everything that was happening in my life suddenly hit me like a ton of bricks. I was a shit father, a practically absent owner, and a dick of a boss to the one person who was trying to keep it all together. Aly haunted my thoughts both day and night and I had no fucking clue what to do about it. My heart was starting to thaw after all this time and it turned out the one person that warmed it was the one person that shouldn't.

I ended up gathering my things and heading out of the office to a little dive bar far enough away to not run into anyone who would know me. I sat at the bar sipping a beer and taking multiple shots of whiskey. Before I knew it, I was sloshed with crazy thoughts whirling around in my head and the ground waving under my feet. I knew I couldn't drive, so I'd called an Uber to take me home, leaving the car parked at the bar.

I crawled out of the bed and forced myself in the shower, letting the hot water rush over me. I was getting too old to wake up with hangovers. Where I used to be able to pop a couple Tylenol and head out for my day, I now felt like I got hit by a bus. Every muscle in my body ached, and every time I moved quickly, I could feel the alcohol swishing around in my stomach. It was miserable, to say the least. When the shower was done, I felt about two percent better, so I changed into a suit for work and headed downstairs to find Aly cooking in the kitchen. She turned to me and shook her head, obviously seeing the pain on my face. I poured myself a cup of black coffee and sat down in the chair for a moment, letting the hot brew flow down my throat.

Aly moved around the kitchen not saying a word, buttering some toast and setting it in front of me. I swallowed hard, the idea of putting food in my stomach more than nauseating. I didn't want to be rude, though, so I picked up a piece and took a bite. I could smell the remnants of the night before on my breath and made myself a note that I needed to brush my teeth again before leaving the house.

"I need you to drop me off at the bar I was at last night when you drop Cooper off," I said. "I left my car there last night and took an Uber home."

I looked up as she walked toward me with the coffee and filled my cup. She stopped and stared down at me with a blank expression on her face. She nodded and turned to put the pot back on the burner. She didn't say a word, and as much as I wanted to hear something from her, anything, I didn't have it in me to push the subject. If I moved, I might hurl all over the place, so talking was out of the question. When Cooper came down, I was glad for the first time in my life that he'd inherited my extreme hatred for mornings and didn't want to say a word.

I sat at the table until they were ready to go. Had I said anything to her the night before? She was way quieter than normal. After breakfast, we headed toward the school. We dropped Cooper off first to avoid questions as to why my car was parked at a bar. I was thankful for Aly's thoughtfulness because it hadn't even crossed my mind. When Cooper was out of the car, and we were on our way to the bar, I cleared my throat and looked over at Aly.

"This is a slightly embarrassing question, but did I say anything to you last night?" I asked.

"No," she said, looking straight ahead, gripping the steering wheel.

As much as I wanted to hear that answer, and as relieved as it made me feel, there was something about her demeanor and shortness that made me feel like she wasn't telling the truth. At the same time, what could I have said that would warrant her lying to me? She hadn't been quiet about anything else up to this point, and I couldn't imagine it would change overnight unless it was really bad. I dropped the subject, though, and decided it was best to move on with my day. She took me to my car and left without another word.

In the office, Inez could see the pained look on my face and chuckled, shaking her head. She had seen me hungover enough times in my life to know when I'd had a rough night before. She brought some bottled water and Tylenol into the office and forced me to take them. Knowing it was for my own good, I agreed. About an hour and three bottles of water later, I was actually starting to feel much better, which was good because Hollis called, and I didn't want him to know I'd been out drinking away my memories.

"Hey, man," he said cheerfully. "I was just calling to catch up."

"Hey," I said, mustering the happiest tone I could. "How are things in Cali?"

"Good, man, really good," he said. "I wanted to make sure you weren't being a dick to my baby sister."

"Me?" I laughed. "I would never."

"Yeah, okay," he scoffed.

"No, for real, ," I said, rubbing my temples. "She's a really good girl, and she's doing wonders for Cooper. I'm glad she's around. Why? Did she say anything different?"

"Nah," Hollis said. "But I know her. She wouldn't tell me if you were. I figured I'd go right to the source and double-check on things. You know I have to."

"Of course. You're the tightest-knit family I've ever met." I laughed.

Hollis switched up the subject and started talking about a girl he'd met at the bar the night before. My eyes wandered off toward the window, and my mind sank back into what had happened in my own life after drowning myself in whiskey and self-pity. Suddenly a flash of something came into my mind, and it made me cringe. Images of me in Aly's room started to come back to me. Images of her in a towel, her hair wet, and me running a finger down her silky, wet shoulder. I shook my head and focused in on the memory, making sure it was that and not a dream I had. But sure as day, I could remember exactly how she smelled, how she felt, and the feeling in my stomach when I touched her. So, I'd confronted her the night before, and not only that, I'd come on to her pretty hard-core.

"Hey, man," I said, interrupting Hollis. "Hey, sorry, can I call you back later? I have another call coming in from a partner."

"Oh, yeah. Sure, brother," he said. "And tell my sister I said hello."

"Will do," I said before hanging up the phone.

I sat staring into space, replaying the moment from the night before over and over again in my head. I could almost smell the sweetness of her body wash in my nose. Should I pretend I didn't remember or apologize for being a drunk ass? At the same time, though, I'd asked her specifically if anything happened, and she'd told me no, point blank. I couldn't wrap my head around why she would lie about something like that. Why wouldn't she come forward and tell the truth about it? She was an adult, I was an adult, and from the memory in my head, she didn't shy away from my touch. You'd think she would have been more than ready to let me know what was going on.

I turned in my chair and propped my elbows up on the desk, planting my face in my hands. I couldn't believe I'd been such an asshole only to turn around and molest my son's nanny in a drunken haze. I almost wished I'd stayed oblivious to what I had done.

"You need more Tylenol?" Inez asked, bringing me a fresh cup of coffee.

"No, but I could use my dignity back, please," I groaned.

Chapter 16

Aly

It was Friday, and a teacher workday at Cooper's school. He was off for the day, and I hadn't even realized it until the night before. Luckily, I hadn't planned anything for the day anyway except continuing with schoolwork. When I went downstairs that morning to prepare breakfast, Cooper was already down there, pouring himself a glass of orange juice. He smiled at me when I walked in the room.

"Hey, Aly," he said.

"Hey, mister. No sleeping in for you today?"

"My friends asked if I could come over and have a video game tournament with them today," he said with a pleading look on his face. "His name is Andrew, and Dad knows their family."

"Okay," I said. "I don't see anything wrong with that, but I have to run it by your father. In the meantime, get me the address so if he says yes, I can put it in the GPS."

"Thank you," he said, running over, hugging me tightly, and then bolting back toward his room.

I laughed and shook my head, walking over and grabbing a cup for coffee. I filled it to the brim and made my way toward Blake's room. I stood there for a moment, thinking about the last time I had been in his doorway and then shook the thought, knocking on his door. He opened up and nodded at me, fixing his tie.

"Your son is off from school today for a teacher workday and is requesting to go over to Andrew's house for a video game tournament with his friends." I smiled, handing him the coffee.

"Thank you." He accepted the cup and took a long sip. "Yeah, sure, that's fine. I just want him home for dinner."

"Okay no problem," I said, leaving and going to tell Cooper the good news.

I dropped Cooper off at Andrew's and headed back home to find the house empty. Blake had already left for work, and I was left with schoolwork to do. However, as I looked around the house, I remembered that Blake had accidentally let the maid service lapse, and the house was a bit of a disaster area, especially since he was terrible at cleaning. I sighed and shrugged my shoulders, deciding to start out by catching up on the loads of laundry overflowing from the baskets in everyone's rooms.

I went to my room, changed into the last clean thing I had, and took my laundry down to the washer. The house was completely empty, so I turned on the stereo in the living room and danced my way back to the laundry room. I was completely oblivious to life at that point, just trying to get through the day without embarrassing myself in one way or another. I got the laundry loaded in and grabbed the detergent, singing into the cap before filling it and dumping it into the machine. Whenever I was home alone at my parent's house, I would do the same thing, only with my iPod. It made the task not so monotonous and boring, and I liked the time to myself. It was stress-free, no worries, and my mind usually worked through my subconscious, clearing out the cobwebs and issues I had packed away for another day.

With everything going on there at the house, it was very much needed. I didn't have any friends to talk to or places to go, so my little laundry dance party was the best I had. It was also exercise, which I'd been slacking on since I didn't know the area and hadn't been going for my normal morning run like I did back in Cali. The fact that it was getting colder outside didn't make it any more motivating.

I closed the lid of the washer and swished my butt back and forth, bobbing around to the music. The only clean thing I had to put on was a tiny pair of spandex shorts and the same tank top Blake had caught me in that night in the kitchen. I turned around, singing to myself, and I stopped dead in my tracks, staring at Blake who was staring back at me, a small smirk on his face. I knew it had to be fate laughing at me. There was no other way around it.

Immediately, I pulled on the bottom of my tank top, trying to make it longer than it actually was. He tilted his head to the side and stared at me, looking up as a slow R & B song played out over the speakers. My cheeks started to glow red, and every excuse in the book started to run through my mind.

"I'm sorry," I chuckled, laughing at my dumb luck. "I thought I had the house to myself, and since you forgot to re-up the maid service, I was trying to get some of the laundry and cleaning done. I figured it was better to do it now than to do it when everyone was here, and there were other things that needed to be taken care of. Cooper was almost out of clean clothes."

I looked back over at Blake, but he didn't say a word. He stared at me with his eyes darkening. Immediately, I felt self-conscious, shuffling my feet beneath me. His face gave nothing away, and I couldn't imagine what he was thinking right then. Suddenly he moved, walking forward slowly and stopping inches away from me. I looked up at him in confusion and nerves, wondering what he was about to say or do. Either it was going to be really good or really bad, but either way, I was in for it. I swallowed hard, smelling the musky scent of his cologne, feeling the heat radiating from his body. It was sensual, and I was starting to feel the heat.

He lifted his hand and ran his finger down the same spot on my shoulder as the other night. I looked up at him, slightly startled. I breathed in deeply, trying figure out if he'd been drinking again, but I didn't smell anything other than his cologne.

"How come you lied to me about the other night?" he asked softly.

"Oh, I, uh, I just thought …" I stumbled terribly over my words.

Before I could open my mouth again to explain, his lips came crashing down onto mine. I could feel the force of his passion behind the kiss, and my knees almost buckled beneath me. My eyes were wide open in surprise, but as he began to move his tongue around in my mouth, I closed them, leaning into him with my body. His breathing escalated with every swirl of his tongue, and all I could think about was him taking me right then and there on the washing machine. It probably was a terrible idea, but I wanted it as badly as he did. I stood there completely unable to move my limbs, caught in his spell.

As he tilted his head to the side, I moaned into his mouth, the lust and want surging through both of us. With that whimper, he groaned, pulling one of his arms around me and running his other hand up my thigh and underneath the edge of my shorts. I arched into him, listening to his groans while he kissed me deeper and deeper with every passing moment. His fingers brushed across my swollen mound, and I ached to feel him inside of me. I wanted him to fuck me so hard, I would scream his name. Everything I'd been feeling for him since I had gotten there all came rushing out as I moved my feet apart to allow him to push deeper under my shorts.

His big strong hand rubbed over my lips and began to separate them, pushing through my wetness, making me whimper and moan even more. He pushed up to my clit and rubbed around it for a moment, making me beg for more. I wanted him to finger me, to make me scream standing barefoot in the laundry room. I wanted everything I'd told myself I wasn't allowed to have, and I wanted it right then. My patience got the best of me, and I reached up, grabbing his shirt and began to untuck it. However, the shift in movement woke him from his trance, and he pulled back, breathing heavily and looking me in the face. We were both heaving, trying to catch our breath, trying to consider the consequences, but it was hard to see through the lust floating around us.

The fact that he wanted me as much as I wanted him turned me on that much more. I never thought Blake would be interested in me like that, but his fingers told a completely different story. He looked at me for a moment, the darkness beginning to dissipate from his eyes.

"God, all the things I want to do to you," he whispered, shaking his head. "But it's wrong."

He let go of me and rushed from the room. I took a step forward in protest, but nothing came out of my mouth. I wanted to change his mind, make him come back, but the moment was lost. He had spooked, looking at me as the nanny and not as the woman who he was about to bend over the dryer five seconds earlier. I put my hand down and backed up toward the chair in the corner of the laundry room. I plopped down, my hands falling haphazardly into my lap. My shoulders slumped forward, and I pouted, feeling like a child who'd lost out on the prize during a game.

My mind was running a million miles a second, and I couldn't focus to save my life. That had been the most passionate and sexual kiss I had ever had in my life. Not to mention the placement of his fingers, which were already heating me at my core. All he did by walking away was make the desire that much more palpable. I wanted him so badly, worse than I'd wanted him before. I could go after him, push him down, and change his mind, but I was not the girl with the confidence for something like that. I was confused as to why, if he was going to go that far, why he wouldn't go all the way. The difference between facing the repercussions of that and the repercussions of him pleasuring my body for hours was very finite in my opinion. Maybe, though, I was being a little irrational, taken in by the moment, wanting more and more. Instead of hot steamy sex, I was left sitting alone in the laundry room, listening to the spin cycle.

Chapter 17

Blake

I walked from the room, clenching my fists to keep myself from turning back and changing my mind. Her kiss. It was so hot. The taste of her lips made my cock even harder just thinking about it. I could feel her perfect, tight pussy right there in my hands, but I'd choked, and for good reason. I marched right up the steps and to my bedroom, locking the door behind me so she didn't follow. If she followed, there was no way I would be able to stop myself again. I didn't think I'd ever wanted a woman so much in my entire life, and it was driving me absolutely crazy.

"Goddamn it," I said out loud, unbuttoning my shirt. "Good job, Blake. Can't keep your fucking hands to yourself."

I cursed and spat angrily as I took off my suit and hung it back on the hanger. I grabbed my cock and shifted it around, wishing the damn thing would get the hint that it wasn't getting any at that moment. I opened the drawer and pulled out some gym clothes, figuring I had to do something to get rid of the tension, emotion, and irritation running through my body. I felt like I was literally about to explode, and I didn't want to do that in front of Aly, especially not after what had happened. She deserved to be treated so much better than that, and I'd acted like she was nothing more than a toy at my disposal. It was horrible of me on multiple levels, and I wasn't sure what to do about that. I may be a hard-ass, but I always made sure to treat a woman with respect. I'd lost control, wanted her so badly, I let my other brain take over.

I shook my head as I sat down on the bed, pulling on my socks. I couldn't believe what I had just fucking done. I couldn't believe how close I had come to pounding into her until we both came hard and loudly. Control had always been one of the things I was best at, but with her, it was like a fight between desire and conscience. It was a foreign feeling to me, something I didn't want to feel anymore. I didn't want to be out of control. I didn't want to be standing there unable to move, unable to force myself to not feel what I was feeling.

I wanted Aly more than anyone I'd ever wanted in my entire life. Her body was calling me all the time. There wasn't a moment when she wasn't around that I wasn't trying to force the thought of putting my hands on her out of my head. Even when I was angry with her, I wanted to fuck her. It was insane on so many levels, like I was a teenager with hormones rushing through me.

Aly had been sexy as hell standing there in that tank top and those little shorts. I couldn't even begin to explain what was going through my head when I saw her dancing. She was both adorable and luscious at the same time. I wanted to kiss her sweetly, but at the same time, I wanted to fuck the hell out of her with force. Everything in me wanted to go downstairs, throw caution to the wind, and take her to bed. But she was so young, so inexperienced in life. If I were to do anything more, there was a definite certainty she would get hurt in some way emotionally. She wasn't used to the world I lived in, and I wasn't sure I could offer her anything more than sex. It wouldn't be fair of me to fuck her and then walk around the house with her, acting like nothing ever happened. That was a dick move, something I'd told myself when I was a kid that I'd never do to a woman, treat her like nothing more than a sexual object for my pleasure.

On top of that, she was Hollis's little sister. If I fucked his sister, and it all turned out terrible, he would literally come to Boston to kick my ass. His family was very close, and he protected her in every way that he could, all the time. We'd been friends our entire lives, and the last thing I wanted was to lose that. He'd been my confidant and strength through most of my life. I didn't have a lot of close friends, but he was one of them, and I didn't want to lose that because I couldn't control my dick. So, now I had to keep my hands off Aly, and the task at hand was going to be even harder than before. I had a taste of her lips, the smell of her body, and I knew what her wet pussy felt like against my fingers. Putting that out of my mind was going to be impossible.

I finished lacing up my shoes and headed down the stairs, turning toward the front door. I took the Mercedes keys off the wall and held them in my hands. I wanted to talk to her about this, I wanted to not leave her feeling rejected and alone in the laundry room, but I was too pent-up. I didn't know if I could control myself if I were to be face-to-face with her again.

"I'm going to the gym," I called out loudly before slamming the door behind me.

I jumped in the car and sped out of the garage and down the driveway to the gate. I sat impatiently waiting for it to open. I needed to put some space between the two of us before I lost control again. I'd already fucked up, and if I didn't get away, I was certain to screw up even worse, and that wasn't my intention. I never intended on hurting her in any way, but that was a real possibility if I didn't get a hold of my hormones. As it was, I might have ruined having a nanny for Cooper.

I hoped she was still going to work for me, that she didn't throw her hands up, pack her bags, and get the hell out of Boston. It wouldn't surprise me if she did. I'd basically assaulted her in the laundry room of my house. Sure, she didn't say no. She'd pushed back into our kiss, and she didn't move my hands, but I was the one who should have been responsible . I was supposed to be the person who looked out for myself, my son, and the people who worked for me, I wasn't supposed to be the person who put any of those people in a questionable situation. If I were her, after watching me run out like a coward, I'd be packing my bags already. But I wasn't her, and she was so different, so much better than I could ever be.

I drove fast down the road, trying to feel the adrenaline taking over, pushing out the need and want in the pit of my stomach. When I reached the gym, I parked quickly in a spot and got out, leaving my bag and everything in the car. I marched right into the workout area and over to the punching bag where I immediately started to attack. I threw punches over and over again, left, right, cross, uppercut. Sweat poured from my forehead as I beat up the bag like it was my own guilty conscience. In my head, I couldn't stop thinking about that kiss, the way her pouty lips felt against mine. Her skin tasted so good, and I wanted so badly to taste the rest of her. Lying her down and licking that soft, wet pussy sounded almost better than the sex itself.

I punched harder, picturing her sprawled across the dining room table, completely naked, her body writhing and pulsating as my tongue slipped through her lips and lapped at her juices. I wanted her so damn badly. I wanted to climb on top of her and lift her legs around me. I wanted to grab that tiny waist and plow my big cock right into her over and over again. I wanted to feel her body as she came all over me, screaming my name, begging me for more. I wanted all those things, but at that moment, all I had was that punching bag and the desire to kick the ever-loving shit out of it.

Aly hadn't pulled away, and she hadn't jumped or paused. She had been totally and completely into it. As soon as the shock of my actions had left her, she folded into me, arching her body against me, opening up and begging me to take her. Maybe, just maybe, because of her desires in return, I hadn't completely scared her away. Maybe she was as intrigued as I was, feeling the magnetism between us. Maybe she was sitting at the house right then thinking about the same things I was, not wanting to leave, not wanting to abandon us even after what happened between us.

All I could do was sit and wait, and during that time, try to get the sounds of her moans out of my head. When she'd moaned into my mouth, I could have come right there. Just the sound of her voice in ecstasy turned me on. It was nuts, and though I liked the feeling, it also made me completely irate at myself. I shouldn't know what her moans sounded like. I should have kept my distance, locked away those desires, but that was easier said than done. I just wanted her so damn badly, I could barely contain it. I growled, throwing another punch into the bag, catching it as it swung wildly back through the air toward my face.

Most people would tell me that with my wealth and status, that I could have anything or anyone I wanted. This, though, was different. Aly was perfect in every way, from her looks, to the way she took care of us, to the huge heart she had on the inside. She was damn perfect, and I couldn't have her. I felt like a child in a toy store being told no by his mother. It made me angry, and I started punching the bag even harder. I took in a deep breath and zeroed in, punching until my hands were hurting. Even then, I didn't stop.

I stayed at the gym for over an hour, punching the bag repeatedly, unable to stop the frustration building inside of me. I worked out until I was so exhausted, my muscles burned from my shoulders to my chest. My hands began to bleed slightly from cracked skin on my knuckles.

I had to center my thoughts, get to a point where I couldn't argue with even myself anymore. I needed to be stern and resolute in my understanding that no matter how much I wanted Aly, I couldn't have her. She was off-limits, and that was the end of it. There were plenty of other women out there for me to get my dick wet with, and she was not one of them.

Chapter 18

Aly

It was Saturday morning, and I was still lying in bed, trying to come to terms with what had happened between Blake and I in the laundry room. It had been sensual, perfect, and I wanted more. But he had run off, telling me it wasn't right, that what he wanted couldn't happen. How could that be? How could two people desire each other so much and have it not meant to be? I was so damn frustrated about the whole thing. I grabbed my phone and dialed my sister Jackie. She would give me good advice or at least listen to what I had to say about everything. I couldn't hold any of it inside me any longer. It was about to drive me crazy.

Jackie and I were close in age, unlike the others. We had basically grown up as a pair until she went off to college, and I was left still in high school as the last lonely child of the household. I loved my other sisters, but they were extremely protective of me. They would never listen to what I had to say and not immediately jump into 'protect little sister' mode. Jackie was the only one of them I trusted with the information. She was the only one who would listen without judgment, not go back to Hollis with it, and would give me solid advice on what to do in the end.

"Hey, sissy," Jackie said, answering the phone. "How's Boston? Meet Matt Damon yet?"

"Ha," I said. "Hardly."

"Why do you sound like something's wrong?" she asked. "Do I need to get the crew?"

"No. God, please, this has to stay between you and me," I pleaded.

"Okay." She chuckled. "What's up then?"

I didn't even realize how much I needed to talk to someone until she asked me what was up. Immediately, I spilled my guts, telling her everything from the sexual chemistry at the airport, to me in my underwear, me walking in on him changing, and then finally to what had happened the day before in the laundry room. She listened carefully, giggling where appropriate. When I was finally done, I felt so much better by getting it off my chest, but I still didn't know what I should do.

"Well, of course, I'm going to tell you first and foremost to not do anything you'll regret," she said. "That being said, you are young and vibrant and you are free to be with whomever you choose. Just make sure it's your decision and be smart about it."

"Oh, it's definitely my decision." Jackie giggled. "On top of that, he's older. I mean, imagine everything you could experience with him. You're an adult now, and I know sometimes with the way Mom and Dad treat you, it doesn't feel that way, but you can make whatever choices are best for you right now. Start living for yourself, girl."

I listened to my sister, thinking about everything that she was saying. In most ways, she was absolutely right. I was an adult, and I had every opportunity to be the woman I wanted to be, not what everyone else wanted me to be. If Blake wanted me and I wanted him, why couldn't we be together?

"Maybe you're right," I said. "Maybe it's time I just go for it and see what happens."

"Yes, see?" she said. "Do what you want to do, not what everyone else wants for you. They mean the best, but they don't always know what the best is."

"Thanks, sis," I said, looking over at the clock as it started to beep. "I gotta go fix breakfast for Cooper."

I got off the phone with my sister and pulled myself out of bed. As I got dressed for the day, I thought about the kiss from the night before, about Blake's reaction, and about how I could be the one to be in control of what happened next. It was obvious he wanted me. So maybe all it was going to take was to show him I was a grown, consensual adult who could make her own decisions. Maybe him seeing me as a woman and not the nanny or Hollis's little sister would change his mind about everything. There was no question in my mind that I wanted him as much as he wanted me. Now, all I had to do was start convincing him it was a good idea.

Just thinking about it put me in a better mood, so I put on my Vans and headed down to the kitchen to make some breakfast. I was only expecting Cooper, but when Blake turned the corner, I blushed, pleasantly surprised. I started the coffee and pulled the eggs and bacon back out of the fridge. It was nice to get to cook for him in the morning.

"Good morning," he said with a smile.

"Morning," I chirped.

"Hey, Aly," Cooper said rounding the corner and stopping when he saw his dad. "Dad! Are you eating breakfast with us?"

"I am," he laughed. "I know. It's crazy, right?"

"I'm glad," Cooper said, smiling at me as I set the plates down on the table. "So, what are we going to do today?"

"Well, I was thinking we could play tourist," he said.

"But we live here," Cooper giggled.

"Yeah, but Aly isn't from here, and I'm sure she wants to see Boston." He smiled. "At least more of Boston than the grocery store and your school. I figured we could make a day of it if you're up to it, Aly."

"Sure," I said, smiling. "I'd love to do that."

"Great," he said. "Then after breakfast, we'll head out."

I was surprised by his change of tone and openness and felt further encouraged to see what might happen. We ate breakfast together, talking about Boston and Cooper's favorite places to go. When we were done, Cooper helped me clean up the kitchen, and we jumped in the SUV and headed out. The first place they took me was the duck boat tour. I had no idea what to expect, but when we got there, I realized how cool it was going to be. We climbed aboard this crazy-looking car that, wildly enough, turned into a boat when we reached the water. The tour took us all over the most famous parts of Boston and ended with a tour of the waterways. It was amazing.

After that, we loaded back up, and Blake drove us over to Faneuil Hall for lunch. When he said where we were going, I expected a restaurant, but when we got there, I realized it was a marketplace. There were people, shops, and restaurants everywhere. Blake and I ended up getting food from Boston Chowda Co. while Cooper opted for Mmmac n' Cheese. We took our food out into the marketplace and found a bench to sit and eat on. It really was an amazing day. We laughed, told jokes, learned about one another, and Cooper was loving it. I couldn't help feeling like we were a family.

That thought, though, I quickly pushed aside. It was a dangerous way to think, and I couldn't get myself caught up in a fairy tale I knew might never come true. When it all came down to it, the day was amazing, but when we got back home, it would be the same as it ever was. They were a broken household, destroyed by the death of their wife and mother.

Still, I didn't want to ruin the day by clouding my mind with those thoughts. This trip was as good for me as it was for them. Every now and then, as we walked along, talking, having a good time, I caught Blake staring at me. It sent butterflies whirling through my stomach and brought that deep red blush right back to my face. Cooper seemed to be in heaven having his dad there with him, and I made sure to get the two of them interacting as much as I could. I asked Blake to tell stories from when he was a kid, talk about his interests, show Cooper that there was more to him than business and sports. I did the same thing to Cooper, trying to get him to open up about himself, let his dad in a little more to the amazing kid he was.

Blake may have planned the trip for me, but I was still there to help bring the family back to normalcy, and there was no way I could take time off from that mission. They both deserved it so much. By the end of the day, I was absolutely exhausted. We walked in the house, kicked our shoes off, and all three of us collapsed on the couch. I curled up in a little ball with my head on the arm of the sofa and smiled. I could fall asleep right there. It had been a long time since I'd done anything that exhausting but fun. I hoped we could continue to do things like that while I was there. Not only was it fun for me, but it brought Cooper and Blake together, which was an amazing thing to watch.

What the two of them didn't realize was that beyond the sports and business, they were very much alike. They were both dreamers, they both wore their hearts on their sleeves, and they both had this glimmer of childhood in their eyes whenever they got excited about something. It was amazing. I wanted them to notice that on their own, and from the looks of it, with Cooper laying his head on his dad's shoulder, it was starting to become apparent.

"All right, Aly is exhausted," Blake said, standing up. "Come on Cooper. You and I are going to cook."

"Really?" Cooper said with a priceless look of excitement on his face.

They walked away, leaving me curled up on the couch, and I smiled. I was going to take every victory while it lasted. In this house, you never knew when the tides could turn.

Chapter 19

Blake

Dinner was a lot of fun, and Aly was right that Cooper was good at cooking. We woke Aly up from her nap to eat and all sat around talking about our day. It was a great way to conclude the tour of Boston. When we were done, Aly volunteered to clean up, and Cooper and I walked into the living room and sat down to read a book together. He was obsessed with Harry Potter like so many other kids his age, so we read a bit of the fifth book, which was one Cooper was reading all over again. He had read the series about four times at that point but never got tired of it.

We sat and read for about an hour until Cooper's eyes began to droop. It had been a big day for all of us, and I knew he was starting to wind down. I closed the book and smiled at him, ruffling his hair.

"Why don't you go brush your teeth and climb into bed?" I smiled.

"Okay." He yawned, standing up and throwing his arms around my neck. "I love you, Dad. Thanks for today."

"I love you too," I said, a twinge in my throat.

He smiled and turned around, walking toward the stairs. I couldn't remember the last time I'd heard those words from him. We'd gotten so far apart that we barely ever said anything like that to each other. I knew it was because of Aly, because of the way she went out of her way to push us together, to make us a family again. I had to thank her.

I went into the kitchen and grabbed a beer, drinking it while I waited for Cooper to get ready for bed. After about twenty minutes, I went upstairs to tuck him in, and found him completely passed out, drooling on his pillow. I chuckled and shut his door before walking down to Aly's room. I knocked, but no one answered, and it didn't look like her light was on. I headed back downstairs and searched around until I found her in the laundry room folding clothes. She had the small stereo in the room on, and she was facing away from me, shaking her perfect ass back and forth as she danced to the music. I smirked, setting my beer quietly on the side table.

I couldn't stop watching her. She was so sexy and so adorable at the same time. She danced to the beat of her own drum, and she didn't care what anyone thought. That was one of the things that attracted me to her the most. She was wild in her own way. After a few minutes, I turned around and closed the door, locking it behind me. As much as I'd told myself I couldn't have her – shouldn't have her – I couldn't hold back any longer.

The sound of the click of the lock made Aly turn around, finding me standing there leaning against the door. Her eyes went wide as she looked from me to the doorknob. She folded the towel in half and placed it on the table in front of her, pulling her headphones from her ears.

"Why did you lock the door?" she asked innocently.

"Because," I said, stalking over to her. "I'm going to thank you for everything you've done."

Before she could protest, I leaned down and kissed her lips. The kiss was soft at first but as I pulled her into me, it deepened. It was as hot and sensual as the night before, only this time, I knew I could take my time. I had no intention of running away scared. I knew exactly what I wanted, and I wasn't going to let my brain talk me out of it again. She reached her arms up and around my neck, opening her mouth and taking my tongue inside. I reached down to her ass and picked her up, wrapping her legs around me.

I pushed my hips forward, grinding my already hard cock against her. She moaned that perfect little moan again, and I completely lost it. I walked forward and sat her down on the counter, kissing her for a moment longer before pulling away. I looked deeply into her perfect blue eyes, the heat rising in my chest.

"Do you want this?" I whispered. "This is your chance to say no."

She nodded and I smiled, leaning back in and kissing her passionately again. The heat between us increased as she lifted her ass from the table and ground against my cock. I groaned, pulling her to me, wanting to feel what she felt like on the inside. I wanted to please her, to show her how much she was appreciated. I ran my hands down over her breasts and pulled her shirt over her head. She reached back and unlatched her bra, pulling it from her shoulders, spilling her perky, round breasts into my hands. I leaned forward and sucked her nipple into my mouth, rolling it around on my tongue. She whimpered, her body poised for me to do whatever I wanted with her.

I stepped back and pulled my polo over my head, flexing my muscles in front of her. She bit her bottom lip and watched me as I slowly unbuckled my pants and let them drop to the floor. I knew she wanted my cock, but I wasn't ready to give it to her yet. I reached down and rubbed my hands over the bulge in my black boxer briefs, showing her how big and hard she had gotten me. She reached out, but I didn't let her touch, smiling as I moved forward and pushed her down on her back. I unbuttoned and unzipped her jeans, pulling them carefully over her perfect curves. She lay there in front of me in a pair of pink string bikini panties, her body perfect in every way.

I rubbed my hand over her hot, wet mound, just over her panties. She groaned, letting her legs fall farther to the sides. I pushed her panties over and slipped one of my fingers slowly inside of her, twisting it as it moved forward. She screamed out, throwing her head back and panting as I watched her face overcome with pleasure. I smiled, pulling my finger back out and stepping forward, rubbing it over her lips, watching her lap and suck it into her mouth. She opened her eyes and looked at me, sending a throbbing straight to my dick. I groaned, wanting to fuck her right then, but pulled back, lowering myself onto my knees. I pulled her forward to the edge of the table and pulled her panties off her, smiling as she grabbed her breasts and stared down at me.

I leaned forward and ran my tongue up through her folds, licking her up to her clit. I reached up and spread her pink plump lips apart and buried my face in her pussy, no longer wasting any precious time. She screamed out, panting in pleasure, reaching down and grabbing onto my hair with her hands. Her hips lifted from the table and ground against my face, and I groaned, tasting her amazing flavor as I pulled my hand back up and pushed two fingers inside of her. She pursed her lips and growled, feeling me fingering her fast and hard as my tongue lapped around her clit, pushing her closer and closer to the edge. I reached up with my other hand and rubbed her clit fast and hard, licking everywhere in between. She slammed her hands down on the table and called out, arching her chest high into the air. I could feel her body tensing as she exploded into orgasm.

I pulled my fingers out and lapped at her juices as they ran out and down my chin. When she had relaxed once again, I wiped my face and stood up, looking down at her with a smile. She shook her head back and forth, laughing and panting at the same time.

She watched with pure lust in her eyes as I pulled off my boxer briefs and stood up straight, my cock long, thick, and hard. I grabbed it with my hand and stroked it a couple of times, my eyes moving over her entire body. I reached forward and lifted her legs up to my shoulders and smiled as I thrust my hips forward hard and fast. She gasped and rolled her eyes, feeling the penetration deep inside of her.

"Fuck," she ground out.

I smiled and began to pump my hips, rolling them hard against her as I thrust my cock deeper inside of her. She reached over her head and held on to the edge of the table, giving me leverage to slam into her over and over again. Her moans echoed through the room, and my cock pulsed as it slid through her tight, wet pussy. I groaned, realizing I might not last as long as I wanted to in the first place. It had been a while, and her pussy was so tight, it squeezed me gloriously.

I pulled out and put her legs down, pulling her from the table. I kissed her hard, flipped her around, and turned her, bending her over the washing machine and grabbing onto that perfect ass. She moaned as I rubbed the head of my cock over her lips, feeling the juices dripping out of her. I wanted to feel her come on my cock so badly. I pushed forward deep inside of her and grabbed onto her waist. At first, I just let loose pounding into her, listening to the sound of our bodies slapping against one another against the dryer. Then, when I felt myself getting closer, I leaned over her, reaching around and rubbing her clit hard and fast as I thrust my hips deeper and deeper.

"I want you to come all over my dick," I whispered.

"Yeah," she moaned in a high-pitched voice.

"You gonna come?" I growled.

"Yeah, fuck me harder. Fuck, yes," she screamed out as I thrust harder against her.

I rubbed her clit faster and faster until she stiffened beneath me, letting loose and shaking in orgasm. She moaned my name, and I groaned when her pussy clamped down hard on my cock. As soon as her juices exploded, running down my shaft, I stood up, pushing as far into her as I could. I groaned, gripping tightly to her, releasing my hot seed inside of her. Our bodies twitched against each other's until finally, we were both done.

I pulled out and smiled, turning her back around and kissing her lips lightly. I picked up her clothes and helped her dress, swatting her on the ass when she was done. She turned around and looked at me with a grin.

"Jesus Aly, you're going to be the death of me," I said.

She raised up onto her tiptoes and pressed a soft kiss to my lips. "But what a way to go, no?"

I threw my head back and laughed. In such a short period of time, the woman had brought so much light into my life it was almost unbelievable. She blushed and scooted out of the laundry room, leaving me standing there by myself. After a couple of minutes, I leaned back against the dryer. How badly had I just screwed up? Whatever the answer, it was worth it.

Chapter 20

Aly

It had been two days, and my body was still tingling from the laundry room sex. It was the hottest fucking thing I'd ever done, and I couldn't wipe the silly grin off my face. Every time I thought about it, butterflies shot into my chest and my pussy got warm all over again. He was so hot, and I'd wanted him so badly, there was no way I was letting my mind talk me out of it. The only worry I had was that we didn't use protection, but I wasn't that concerned about it. He was a widower who I was pretty sure hadn't been with anyone in the past year, and it had been longer than that for me. Neither one of us had any diseases, and as far as pregnancy was concerned, I'd been on the pill for years. All our ducks seemed to be in a row, and now it was only a concern for me what happened next.

I finished up what I was doing downstairs and headed up to work on some schoolwork. I had already gotten Cooper off to school, and Blake had left early for work. When I got up there, I started to think about things. Had I taken my pill that morning? It was so automatic usually that I didn't have to think about it. I was sure I had, but for peace of mind, I went to the bathroom and checked the pack.

As soon as I opened it, my heart fluttered in my chest. Fuck. I had forgotten two days in a row to take the damn things. Back home, I worked on a schedule I had been following like clockwork for years. Here, at Blake's house, I was just getting used to the routine. I had been so distracted with my new life, I'd completely blanked. I popped the pills out of the package and took them both, unsure if that would actually work, but I wasn't taking any chances. I shook my head, slightly disappointed in myself. I was the responsible girl who didn't take chances, and there I was off in La La Land acting like I had nothing to lose.

After that, I went back to the normal routine I'd set for myself based on Cooper's schedule. Several days had passed, and I found myself wanting Blake again and again. He was ground into brain along with visions of what we'd done in that laundry room.

Every time I went near there, my heart quickened, and I lost my breath. It was strange, though, ever since that day we had barely spoken a word to each other, and when we did, it was generally in passing. The recognition of that fact made my heart drop, and I wondered if he was regretting sleeping with me. Was he done with me? Had he gotten exactly what he wanted and then decided to turn into a ghost? The not knowing was driving me crazy, and I thought about what my sister had told me.

I was a strong, independent woman, and I needed to stand up for what I wanted. I deserved an answer to what was going on, and I wasn't going to sit around and wait for it. Life was too short, too wavering, for me to go through that kind of agony day in and day out. I wanted answers, and I wanted them sooner than later. I told myself the next day I would confront him and find out exactly what was going on.

The next morning came quicker than I expected, and I woke up with nerves blowing through me. The first thing I had to do was get Cooper ready for school and dropped off. I went to the kitchen and cooked breakfast, trying to slow myself down and calm the anxiety that was taking me over. Cooper was quiet, but he usually was in the morning, and we ate together like we always did. When he was done eating, I cleaned up the kitchen and went out to the SUV to wait for him. The other car was still there, so I knew Blake was still home.

"Have a great day," I yelled to Cooper as he got out of the car at school and waved back at me.

I smiled and headed back to the house, hoping to talk to Blake before he left for work. I parked the SUV in the driveway and jogged inside, making my way to his home office. He wasn't there, so I went upstairs thinking maybe he'd stayed home for the day, but he wasn't there either. He'd left before I got back from dropping Cooper off. I had to admit I was more than a little disappointed I couldn't clear up the whole thing before starting my day. The questions were killing me.

I went downstairs, poured myself a cup of coffee, and took my time drinking it. I sat at the kitchen table contemplating the whole situation over and over until I was sick of thinking about it. When I was done, I got up and decided to do a little housecleaning, which usually helped clear my mind. I pulled out the vacuum and went over the entire lower level, finding myself meticulously cleaning every corner and as far up the walls as the hose could reach.

I grabbed my phone from my room and called my mom, remembering suddenly that I'd completely forgotten to do that. She was going to be upset that I didn't call sooner, but I had a lot going on and my mom was not the person I could talk to about it. The phone rang several times and just before it went to voice mail, she picked up.

"Well, hello, stranger," she said. "Nice of you to drop a line."

"I know. I suck," I said. "I'm so sorry. Things here have been crazy, and with school and early mornings, I've been exhausted. How are you guys?"

"We're good," she said. "Livin' the childless couple life."

"I'm sure." I laughed.

"You know, walking around naked, doing whatever we want," she said.

"Ew, Mom. Ew," I replied with a chuckle.

I talked to my mom for close to an hour, getting updated on all the latest drama with my sisters and whoever they happened to be dating at the time. When I got off the phone with her, I grabbed my laptop and brought it downstairs to the dining room table. I opened it up, ready to get some work done, when the doorbell rang. I groaned and pulled myself out of the chair, walking to the front door and opening it quickly.

"Hi," I said, staring at a delivery man carrying a huge bouquet of flowers.

"Hi, I have a delivery for Aly," he said with a smile.

"That's me." I smiled, taking the vase from him.

I signed a slip and thanked him, closing the door and carrying the flowers into the dining room. They were gorgeous, red and white roses with lilies stuck in-between, my favorite flower. I reached in and pulled out the card, opening it up and smiling. It read, "In case my other way of thanking wasn't good enough." I threw my head back and laughed, feeling so much better than I had when I woke up that morning. He had gone out of his way to make sure I knew he was thinking about me.

I shook my head and smiled, thankful that the stress of that was over with. I closed my laptop and put it under my arm, grabbing the flowers and heading to my room. When I got up there, I was almost as giddy as a school girl. I set my laptop on the bed and perfectly arranged the flowers on the dresser in front of the mirror. I stepped back and smiled, staring at them with adoration. No one had ever sent me flowers before, and I didn't think anyone had ever gotten some that were that beautiful. I grabbed my laptop, opening it up and sitting cross-legged on the bed, and started my schoolwork. Every now and then, I glanced up at the vase and smiled big, excitement in my chest.

Somewhere in the back of my mind though, a tiny voice said it was dangerous for me to get too excited about what was going on. The flowers weren't a proposal, and they didn't mean anything else would happen between us. Still, I was tired of talking myself out of being happy to err on the side of caution. I shook the doom and gloom away and continued working on schoolwork until it was time to pick up Cooper.

As usual, when I got there, he was all smiles and happy, a completely one-eighty from where he was whenever I dropped him off. He jumped in the car and threw his bookbag in the back, looking over at me with a smile. I grinned and gave him a confused face.

"What are you so happy about?" I laughed.

"I don't have any homework tonight," he said. "It's like a miracle."

"That's awesome." I laughed. "Then we have to do something special. Let's go get ice cream!"

"Yes," he said, bouncing up and down. "I know the perfect place, and I can tell you how to get there."

"All right, let's do this."

He navigated us through the city and closer to the house to an ice cream place on the corner of a long row of shops. We found a parking spot and walked happily toward the shop, talking loudly about his day. When we got inside, I actually started to get excited. It was all homemade ice cream, every topping you could imagine, and it looked like an old-timey ice cream parlor. We both picked out two scoops and took our ice cream over to a table by the window.

"This is a great day," Cooper said, excited. "I hope Dad comes home for dinner. That would make it even better."

"It would, wouldn't it?" I laughed.

"Aly?" Cooper said, quieting down.

"What's up?" I said, concerned.

"I'm really glad that you came," he said. "At first, I hated the idea of having a nanny, I thought you would be a mean old lady with a big nose and mean voice. But that isn't at all what you are. And you make my dad and I get along better. I think he likes to spend time with me now. It's like the old times when Mom was alive."

"Of course, he likes you. He loves you," I said. "And I'm happy I can help you guys get back into a comfortable life. I know things have been so stressful, but that doesn't mean it will always be like that."

He smiled and nodded his head, taking a big bite of his ice cream. I laughed and did the same thing. I was pretty sure I just figured out what I wanted to write about for my school paper. Family dynamics seemed to be such a strong subject, and it affected the way a child was raised. I was on the ground floor of it, too, and I could really knock this one out of the park.

Chapter 21

Blake

I stared at the computer screen, my mind on a completely different planet. Every so often, I tapped the mouse or typed a few letters into the empty email on the screen to make Inez think I was working. The last thing I wanted to see was that look of pity she'd finally stopped giving me. I couldn't concentrate, though, not even for five minutes. Aly was on my mind night and day, her face, her voice, her laugh, and her moan echoed through my conscience. I'd been avoiding her since the hot night in the laundry room, and I wasn't even sure why. It seemed like what I should do. I had made a mistake, but for some reason, it didn't feel like one. It felt like an itch that had only partially been scratched, and while I was thinking about how I'd made a bad choice, I was also thinking about how I wanted to do it all over again.

I had been with several different, beautiful women in the past, but no one had that effect on me. I was incapable of bringing myself to completely throw away the idea of being with her again. The only thing I knew to do to keep myself out of trouble was to stay away from her. Obviously, though, that was not working, and I was back in a position where I was anything but productive. I was the opposite. I was destructive in my progress with both my company and my son and all because I couldn't come to terms with how much I wanted that woman. She was so familiar, so warming, and I was attracted to her like I'd never been before.

I'd sent her a beautiful bouquet of flowers not only because I did want to thank her but because I didn't want to hurt her by dipping out like I was. She had thanked me for the flowers in a chance crossing in the kitchen, but other than that, I'd made it a point to stay away from her. I left for work either before she got up or while she was taking Cooper to school, I said barely anything during dinner, and afterward, I locked myself away to keep my distance. The thing that really got me, that baffled me the most, was that I was a grown ass man. I should have been able to control myself in any situation, much less one that involved a woman who was off-limits. There was something about her, though, that pulled me in and wouldn't let go, no matter how much I needed to.

I found myself lying awake at night thinking about her several doors down, wondering if I should sneak into her bed. She was like a magnet to me, and I didn't know how to break the connection.

I sighed and turned off my computer, leaning back in my chair and turning toward the window. I had the office with a view because I put blood, sweat, and tears into this company, and now I couldn't even get through a dozen emails. I'd never been so twisted up over a girl in my life. I needed things to settle, to be in control again, to make my own choices because it was what I wanted, not what everyone else thought was right or wrong. I shook my head and stood up, knowing there was no way I was going to get anything done that day. I needed to go work out or do something to get my mind calmed. I looked up at Inez as she sat back at her desk.

"Hey," I said, walking to my door. "I'm going to head out early. I need to go to the gym, and then I'll check in from the home office."

"You're the boss, boss," she smiled, not noticing my mental discomfort.

I smiled and went back in my office, grabbing my coat and keys and then heading out. I got in my car and drove through the garage, thinking about my workout. When I got on the road, my motivation diminished significantly. I no longer had any interest in going to the gym. By the time I reached the turnoff, I'd talked myself into working out at home. When I got there, I parked the car in the garage, and my motivation had further gone from a heavy workout to going up to my room, putting on pajama pants, and watching terrible daytime television. I wasn't in the right mindset for anything, I guessed.

Once I was inside, I slipped off my shoes and walked into the living room. Everything was cleaned and picked up like always, and I knew Aly was around there somewhere. I really needed to get the maid service back. It wasn't fair that the nanny also be the one picking up after us all and even doing Cooper's and my laundry on a regular basis, though I didn't mind watching her clean. One thing I didn't mind at all was walking around the corner to find her sexy body, barely clothed, bouncing around.

Standing in the living room, I heard a clang coming from the kitchen. I assumed that was where I would find Aly. I walked into the room and stood in the doorway, staring at Aly at the kitchen sink. She wasn't wearing the shorts I loved, but she was wearing a perfect yellow dress that showed off her toned and shapely legs, including half of her thigh. She looked so sexy standing there, listening to her music, washing the dishes, swaying her hips back and forth. She had no idea I was standing behind her staring, and I liked it that way.

Immediately, I could feel my pants tighten and my rational thoughts left me. I wanted to walk up to her and bend her right over the sink, grabbing her by the shoulders and fucking her over the sudsy water. The dress had me from the moment I walked into the room, and I could not be held liable for how I reacted toward her.

All day long, I had chastised myself for sleeping with her, only to go home and throw all of that out the window, staring at her sexy hips and the way the back of her skirt flipped up with every sway of her body. I threw caution to the wind. There was no way I could keep my hands off her any longer. I walked up behind her and grabbed her hips, looking down at her sexy, tight ass. She turned her head and looked up at me, pulling out her earbuds and smiling. She was so gorgeous with her light makeup, fresh smile, and rosy cheeks.

Her body felt right in my hands, like all the stress from before had melted away with her touch, like I was right back exactly where I was supposed to be. The house was quiet since Cooper was at school and having this little barefoot beauty standing in front of me was almost idyllic. She was this force to be reckoned with, someone who fueled this strange fire inside of me. As I studied her, I had never felt more at home with a woman in my life, and though it was an uneasy feeling for me, I couldn't walk away at that moment.

"Hi there." She smiled.

Her smile gleamed under the glow of the fluorescent light above the sink. Her perfect blue eyes sparkled like the crisp ocean waves of the beaches in the islands. The scent of lavender and vanilla wafted from her cool, clean skin. I was about to lose control. Normally, I would answer her back with strength and resilience, but nothing came out of my mouth. All I wanted to do was kiss those perfect red lips, run my hands over that perfect white skin, and feel the passion of that perfect wet pussy.

I leaned down and nipped at her bare shoulder for a moment, kissing it before nibbling with my teeth once again. She put the dish back in the sink and grabbed the towel, wiping the suds from her hands. She turned in my grasp, leaning her body back against the sink and looked at me with curiosity. She had a smirk on her lips, like she knew she didn't want to stop but she had to question the change of action I was showing. I wanted to shush her before she could speak. I wanted to keep that moment absolutely perfect, just like she was, but that would be nearly impossible after how far I had pulled away.

"I thought we weren't doing this again," she said with a coy smile.

"I'll be honest," I said. "I know coming on to you, being with you is wrong. I know that. The age difference, the fact that you're my son's nanny, you're my best friend's little sister, and on and on, but at the end of the day, I can't get you off my mind. The other night in the laundry room was impulsive, I know, and I know I hid away from it, but seeing you standing here in the middle of the kitchen like this is making things incredibly hard to turn away from. I don't know what it is about you, Aly, but I can't seem to help myself when I'm around you. There's a light that draws me, and I am so completely and lost in you."

"Wow." She smiled. "That was quite the answer."

"You asked the question," I said, standing close, the draw of her lips like a drug.

She arched her hips to meet mine, a coy smile moving across her face. I rubbed my hands up her waist and back down to her hips, pressing her hard against my already hard cock. I bit my lip and let my hands run down her body, taking in every inch of naked skin that was revealed to me.

"I feel the same way Blake. I always have. I want you so bad it hurts."

"Then let me make you feel better," I said, grasping her tightly and setting her up on the counter.

Chapter 22

Aly

When I was listening to music while washing the dishes, I never thought in a million years I would feel Blake's hands wrapped around my waist like this. I never actually thought I would feel Blake's hands wrapped around my waist at all ever again, but there I was, his arms around me, him staring down at me with his dark turned-on eyes. It was erotic, standing barefoot in his kitchen, his hands grasping at the soft fabric of my dress, his face depicting a man who knew exactly what he wanted no matter how hard he'd been trying to hold back. I loved that he wanted me so badly. I never knew what it felt like to have someone want me, to lust after me in ways I could have never imagined before. I wanted him in a way that I couldn't even put into words, and though I knew it might end in nothing more than heartbreak and sorrow, at that moment, I didn't care.

Sitting on the kitchen counter, I reached for the straps of my dress, but he stopped me, a smile on his face. He didn't get me naked at all, he simply dropped down, pushing his hands up my thighs and spreading my legs far apart. I leaned back, resting my head on the cabinet and holding firmly to the cold granite counter below me. He pushed my panties to the side and dipped his head down, parting my plump lips with his fingers. I gasped loudly as his warm, wet tongue met my skin. Passion pulsated through me. It was insane that he could make me feel this way with a flicker of his tongue, but already, he had me perched on the edge of ecstasy.

His mouth smoothed over me like a wave, rocking his tongue back and forth against my clit and then moving down and back up again. I clenched to the granite top, leaning my head back and moaning loudly, my eyes shut, my mind taking in every feeling he was giving me. It was like he knew just how to rub me, just how to roll me through the pleasure, and I loved every moment of it.

I looked up as he reached onto the counter and grabbed the coconut oil I had been cooking with. He opened the top and smirked up at me, sending chills through my entire body. I watched as the oil poured out over his fingers, lubricating them. He stood up and pulled me from the counter, turning me around and lifting my skirt. He sank low again and positioned himself between my legs and the counter, lapping at my pussy once again. He pulled my panties to my ankles and barked his order.

"Bend over on the counter," he said with an authoritative tone.

Who was I to question that kind of passion? I bent over and rested my head on the counter, feeling him pull my clit into his mouth. His hand smoothed over my ass as he pushed my feet further apart. Slowly, he pushed a finger into my ass, forcing a gasp from my throat. It was pleasure and pain all wrapped up in one perfect and seductive package. I moaned loudly, throwing my head back as he began to finger my ass, his mouth still moving rapidly over my wet, pulsating pussy. It was so hot, I could barely stand, my knees beginning to shake beneath me.

"Have you had it like this before?" he asked in a soft growling tone.

"No," I gasped.

"Do you like it?"

"Yes," I screamed out as he pushed a second finger into my tight hole.

He went slowly at first, gliding his fingers in and out as he licked and sucked on my clit. I groaned in ecstasy, wanting more and more, signaling to him to move faster. My mind was completely jumbled, taking in every sensation that blew through my body. The heat in my stomach had expounded, and the pressure building inside of me was like nothing I had ever felt before. I pulled my hand down in front of me and grabbed his hair, tilting my hips into him. He pushed his face up and down through my juices, groaning as I gripped tighter. My calves shook as I lifted up on my toes and back down again, grinding my pussy against his face. I could feel the orgasm teetering on the edge of explosion, but I held back, wanting to experience the ecstasy a bit longer.

"I want to taste you come," he whispered between the sounds of his lips smacking against me.

"Yeah?" I wailed.

"Come for me, right here in my mouth," he ordered. "Mmmm, come on, baby."

The sound of his voice was erotic and only aroused me further. I screamed out, lifting my top half up on my hands, tilting my head back as my body began to move in waves over his face. He picked up the pace with his fingers, fucking my ass with tenderness but purpose. I never thought I would have his fingers in me like that, but it was the most pleasurable thing I had ever felt. He reached up with his other hand and grabbed onto my ass cheek, growling deeply as he pulled my pussy into his mouth and moved his head back and forth. As his tongue slapped against my clit, I couldn't hold back any longer.

My mouth fell open, and I screamed out in pleasure as the orgasm that was trapped in my belly exploded outward, sending waves of ecstasy through every muscle in my body. It was unlike anything I had ever felt, and I closed my eyes, holding my breath until it had completely washed over me. As it dissipated, he pulled his fingers out but kept his mouth firm, slowly licking my pussy. I shuddered at his touch, electricity vibrating from my clit.

He pulled back, scooting out from under me and standing up. I stood with my head hanging, trying to catch my breath. He chuckled as he moved next to me and rinsed the oil from his hands. I stood up and reached down, pulling my panties back up and my skirt down. I handed him the towel and shook my head, watching him enjoying my inability to even think at that moment.

"You're welcome," he whispered, kissing me on the cheek. "Do you need me to drive or do you have it?"

"Mmmm." I lifted my hands and shook my head. "I got it. Just give me a moment."

"I'll be here when you guys get back," he whispered, kissing me on the cheek again and walking from the room.

I looked up with my mouth hanging open in shock and awe and then smiled, straightening myself out and grabbing the keys from the counter. I had to go get Cooper, and I had never been happier that I had to drive there to get him. In the car ride over, I could hear my heart beating in my ears. My mind flickered through the memories of what Blake had done with me, sending butterflies flittering through my entire body. My stomach dropped but not in a bad way, in a way that made me want to do it again and again and again. I couldn't believe what had just happened.

It was like I was living in some kind of crazy porno or alternative life. During the day, I did laundry, did homework, and prepared meals, but every so often, this man would blow through my life like a hurricane. He would tumble me about, showing me things I had never even thought of doing in my wildest fantasies. It was unbelievable to me that I, this shy and quiet girl from the San Francisco Bay area who never really did anything other than missionary with guys who really had no idea what they were doing, ended up in some sexual fantasy world with a man who I couldn't seem to get enough of.

I knew when I got there and saw him that between his age and his confidence, he could knock me right off my feet with his sexuality, but I never thought it would be this insane. He was so good at what he did. He knew exactly where to touch me, exactly how to touch me, and just what to say to get me going. He had gotten me off and asked for nothing in return, which was mind-blowing to me. Every guy I had ever been with was worried about one thing and one thing only, getting their rocks off as fast as they could. Not Blake. He took his time, almost lived and breathed off of watching the pleasure roll through me. It was hot and tantalizing and dangerous all at the same time.

All the new things he could show me lit a fire in me that wasn't there before. Suddenly, my explorative side was in full effect, and I wanted to know everything, every trick up his sleeve. I wanted him to use my body for pleasure, show me exactly what sex was really about. The laundry room sex that we'd had was the hottest thing I'd done to that point, and I didn't think it could get any better than that, but he was definitely proving me wrong. He made the best out of a tight space and sent me reeling. Then, to come into the kitchen and touch me like he did, his mouth so warm against me, his fingers careful and strong at the same time, it was something I couldn't fully wrap my head around. I couldn't even imagine how it would be if he ever decided to take me in his bed.

The passion that would ensue in a situation like that would be otherworldly. If he had the time to do whatever he wanted, I didn't know if I would be able to get back out. I might decide to stay there forever, waiting for him to come back to bed each day, waiting for those strong hands to take over and push me into another sexual dimension. That was it, too, those hands. They were so right, almost as if they had a mind of their own. They moved meticulously over my body, in sync with his mouth and his desires.

He was so domineering, taking control of me, making me enjoy every moment. I loved how he ordered me around, how he expected me to listen to him. It was so hot, and every time I heard his voice, I wished it was saying those things to me over and over again. I surrendered whenever I was in his hands, and that jolt of masculine power it gave him only turned back around and translated into unbelievable pleasure for me.

As I pulled up in front of the school in the car line, I was glad to see Cooper wasn't outside yet. I had to get myself together before he got into the car. I had to push the thoughts of what happened onto the back burner and move on with the day. It was going to be incredibly hard to do, but by nightfall, I would be able to live that feeling all over again and hopefully more.

Chapter 23

Blake

Cooper was in bed and had been there for about an hour. I sat on my bed, the door cracked open, watching the light under Aly's door flicker as she walked around. I held tightly to the book in my hand, not reading it, using it as a distraction, a way to make myself feel okay about the fact that I couldn't stop thinking about her body. I wanted to give her more of what I'd given her that afternoon, only I wanted it to completely blow her out of the water. I wanted to shake her mind, push her to the edge, and then send her reeling over like nothing she'd ever experienced.

After about ten more minutes, I scooted to the edge of the bed and listened for any sign that Cooper was still awake. The house was silent, so I crept out of my room and pulled his door shut all the way. Carefully, I tiptoed down the hall to Aly's room, standing in front of it, smiling at myself, knowing I had finally given up my inhibitions. I carefully and quietly knocked on the door. Her light footsteps approached, and I stood up straight as the door slowly opened. She looked at me with a smile and backed up as I stepped forward, letting myself into her room. Once inside, I watched as she leaned back against the poster bed, watching my every movement. I turned and closed the door carefully, locking it and staring at the wood frame for a moment before turning back around to face her.

There was a nervousness on her face, but it was mixed with an excitement I hadn't seen in her before. She liked what I was doing to her, and from the way she tapped her foot, I could tell she was ready for more. Slowly, I walked over to her and wrapped my arm around her waist, looking deeply into her eyes. I raised my other hand up and showed her the bottle of lube that I had brought over. She smirked and raised an eyebrow, playing coy with me, and I loved it. She reached up to take the bottle, but I pulled it behind my back, leaning in and kissing her lips sensually and slowly.

"And what is that for?" she asked, as I pulled away.

"That's for me to know and you to find out," I whispered.

"Mmmm." She shivered, leaning in and kissing my lips.

I loved showing Aly things for the first time. It was hot and sensual. And I especially loved how she immediately submitted to me without even asking her to do so. She gave her body to me and let me bring her the pleasure I could. I set the lube down on the bed and grabbed the bottom of her skirt, slowly lifting it up and over her head. I grabbed her tits with both hands and massaged them strongly, setting the mood for my dominance. She moaned softly, leaning her head back against the bed and rolling her eyes back. I leaned forward and ran my lips across her chest before standing back up and grabbing her tightly with one hand around the waist. She bit her lip as I pushed her panties to the floor and spun her around, pushing her down on the bed.

I rubbed my hands down her back and to her ass, massaging her ass cheeks roughly. She reached up and stretched her arms out in front of her, grabbing onto the comforter and looked back at me with her seductive stormy blue eyes. I growled and stood up, pulling down my pants and tossing them to the side. She bit her lip, watching me undress, running her eyes over every inch of skin as it was revealed. I pulled my boxer briefs down to the floor and grabbed onto my bobbing cock. I stood there for a moment, rubbing my hand up and down the shaft, staring her deeply in the eyes before grabbing the lube and squirting it all over my dick.

"Don't be nervous," I whispered, feeling her back tense under my hand. "I'll be gentle."

I stepped toward her and guided my cock over her ass, rubbing the lube in deep. I grabbed her hips and slowly began to push, watching her push her face down onto the bed. I moved slightly inside, stopping and letting her breathe before pushing again. Over and over I did this until my cock was halfway inside of her. I started there, slowly bringing it back and then forward again. She breathed deeply, her eyes closed, and moved slowly until her body relaxed. She let out a small moan, muffled by the comforter, and I knew she was enjoying herself.

"Relax for me," I cooed, moving forward and then back again.

She gripped the comforter again but this time in lust, tilting her head back and closing her eyes, a look of passion on her face. I gripped her tighter and began to move faster and deeper, leaning forward and kissing her shoulders. She gasped, leaning her head back and growling. As the moment heated, I pushed deeper, filling her with my cock, stretching her just enough to give her the perfect sensation. Low moans escaped her mouth, and she covered it, trying to be quiet for Cooper.

I wanted so badly to let loose, but I waited for her, waited for her to want it that badly too. Slowly, I reached around her and cupped her wet, pulsing pussy, rubbing gently. She breathed deeply, trying to hold back her screams as I swirled my fingers through her mound. She put both of her palms down on the bed and raised her top half up. I wrapped one arm around her waist and helped stabilize her as I pushed up on my toes, pressing my cock deep into her ass. My other hand stayed on her pussy, slipping down until I could push two fingers inside of her. She clapped her hand over her mouth and muffled a scream, her body moving in motion with mine.

It was so hot, so erotic, and I had to hold back from coming. I slowed the pace for a moment to capture my bearings, but she wasn't having it. She moved her body up and down my shaft, thrusting her ass outward as she pushed up on her toes and then lowered herself back down. I growled, letting go of my control, grabbing onto her waist tightly and slamming myself up inside of her. She moaned again in need, digging her nails into my arm as I pushed her closer to release. I leaned forward and pursed my lips next to her ear.

"You like it?" I asked.

"God," she whispered. "I'm gonna come."

I smiled and wrapped my arm around her waist, bobbing her up and down on my shaft. I groaned, leaning my head back as she bit her lip and held back her screams. Suddenly, her body went stiff. She was tipping over the edge. I reached back down and feverishly rubbed her clit, watching her whole body begin to shake. I growled and fucked her faster and harder, allowing myself to let go. She lurched forward, bending at the waist, letting out a single bellow as my cock pulsated inside of her, releasing my hot seed.

We stayed in that position until every ounce of pleasure was expunged, holding tightly to one another. I pulled out, and she collapsed onto the bed, slowly pulling herself toward the pillow. I smiled and crawled up next to her, pulling her up on my chest. We laid there, her fingers tracing my tattoos quietly, whispering to one another.

"I think its best we don't tell Cooper," I said, hoping for a good reaction.

"Oh, I agree," she said. "He wouldn't understand, and I don't want him to get hurt in any way."

"Thank you," I replied, kissing her forehead.

"How is work?" she asked. "Have you gotten back into the flow of things better?"

"I don't know," I sighed, keeping one arm wrapped around her shoulder and the other tucked under my head. "I've been floating for so long now, hovering through life right above the survival line since my wife died. Of course, it's hard to lose a spouse, but what I don't tell many people is that when she died, she did so in the arms of the lover I didn't know she had."

I usually kept that information to myself, not wanting people to talk, but Aly was so easy to confide in. I could trust her to keep a secret like that close to her heart, no matter what happened between us. She was an amazing woman, that was for sure, and part of me wanted to open up to her, let her into who I was, what I struggled with, and what I thought about on a daily basis.

"Oh Blake. How awful for you. I'm sorry it happened like that. I can only imagine how painful that must be for you. That being said, you will have to eventually let go of this anger, Blake. You're letting it take over your life, and when you do that, it not only harms you, but it harms Cooper too, and that's not something he can really understand. He wants his happy father back. He's ready to move forward in life, but he can sense the tension, and it strongly affects him."

"I know," I sighed. "And you're so spot on. How did you get so smart so young?"

"I know compared to your old ass, I seem young," she said, poking me playfully in the side. "But I'm twenty-three now, and in the grand scheme of things, that isn't so young."

"You know, I thought you were younger than that," I said. "But even still, there's a huge age difference between the two of us. That doesn't bother you?"

"No it doesn't. Blake, I've wanted you for as long as I could remember. I don't care about the numbers."

We lay there for a while talking about life and then fell asleep together, her wrapped up in my arms. I woke before the sun rose, listening to the birds chirping out the window. Cooper would be waking soon, and I didn't want to leave, but it would be for the best. I scooted out of bed and pulled on my clothes, looking down at the blonde beauty sprawled out under the covers. She took my breath away for a moment, and as my eyes moved down the dip in her back all I could think about was climbing back in bed and having my way with her over and over again.

Chapter 24

Aly

Saturday flew by, and though I was technically off, I spent my time lounging around with the guys, cooking light meals, and watching movies. It was nice doing something normal and calm for once. That night, Blake and I slept separately, but not without him giving me a passionate kiss before bed. My heart fluttered every time I was near that man, and it was driving me crazy in a good way. Sunday morning, I got out of bed early to make some muffins for the guys. I stood, stirring the batter, thinking about Blake, daydreaming about my life there, and pretty much sitting on cloud nine, dangling my feet over the edge.

Right before it was time to put the muffins in the oven, there was a knock on the door. I furrowed my brow. Who would be showing up like this on a Sunday morning? I grabbed the towel and wiped my hands before heading over and opening the door. I stopped dead in my tracks, excitement flying through me at the sight of Hollis standing in front of me with a big smile on his face.

"Surprise." He laughed.

"Yes, it is," I said, reaching for him and hugging him tightly. "What are you doing here?"

"I missed my little sis. Is everyone else awake?"

"No, they're still sleeping," I said, shaking my head in shock.

"Good. Come on. Let's go grab some breakfast and catch up," he said, nodding to his car.

"Yes, of course," I said, taking off my apron. "Let me slip on my coat."

We headed out to a small diner across town and sat talking about life and what had been going on. I missed my big brother so much, and I loved having him there, but I was trying desperately hard not to give away that Blake and I were sleeping together. He had a nose for these things, so I had to make sure I didn't overly excite myself talking about him.

"Do you like your new job?"

"I love it." I smiled.

"I knew you would," he said. "I knew it would take you letting go and coming out here, and you would see how much you love it. I see a change in Blake too. He's actually working again."

"Oh, I think that has more to do with the release of stress from always worrying about Cooper." I smiled, feeling nervous.

"That and my baby sister has a way of brightening everything she touches," he said, putting a bite of food in his mouth.

"So, how are the others?" I asked, wanting to change the subject.

He rolled his eyes and took in a deep breath before going into all the constant drama with my sisters and their boyfriends or dates or whatever they were. I had sent Blake a text letting him know where I was, and apparently, he knew all about the surprise. When we were done with breakfast, we headed back to the house to see everyone.

"Uncle Hollis," Cooper said excitedly, running and hugging him.

"Hey, buddy," he said, bending down. "How are you? You look like you've grown a foot."

"I'm good," he said. "And its three inches, to be precise."

"Uh-oh, you're gonna be shaving soon," he said, poking Cooper in the belly.

"No," Cooper giggled.

"Hey, old friend," Blake said, hugging Hollis tightly. "It's really good to see you."

"You too," Hollis said. "And with a smile on your face."

"Things are getting better," Blake said, shifting his eyes momentarily toward me.

"Are you ready to go over that stuff we talked about?" Hollis asked.

"Oh, yeah." Blake turned to me. "Would you mind hanging out with Cooper for a bit? Your brother and I have some business to talk about, and Cooper would be bored out of his mind."

"Of course. We can go bake some cookies." I smiled, reaching my hand out for Cooper.

Cooper pouted but then smiled, taking my hand and walking back to the kitchen with me. I pulled out a recipe card for almond sandies and set it in front of him. He picked up the card and read all the instructions before walking over and turning on the oven.

"You think you got this one while I watch?"

"Pfft," he said, waving his hands. "Are you kidding? This is easy peasy."

Cooper was a natural when it came to cooking. As soon as he was familiar with the tools, he worked his way around a kitchen like he'd been doing it for years. I knew the sandies wouldn't really be a challenge, but I wanted something calm and fun for us to do. He kept asking me for harder and harder recipes, so I had been making a book of them and picking one each time we came to cook together.

"I didn't know Uncle Hollis was your brother," he said as he mixed the ingredients in the bowl.

"Yep, and we have three other sisters too." I smiled.

"Wow, that's a big family," Cooper said. " I've always wanted a brother or sister."

"You do?" I asked.

"Yeah."

"Well having siblings is cool most of the time. Except when they steal your stuff."

Cooper giggled as he added another ingredient into the bowl and stirred with the whisk the way I had showed him when we started cooking together. He was so sweet, and I could now see his father in his eyes and his motions. When Blake was shut up inside of himself, it was hard to see, but once he started to relax and smile again, I could definitely tell Cooper was his father's son. Just then, Hollis and Blake turned the corner back into the kitchen, shaking hands.

"That was fast." I smiled.

"We talked about everything over the phone, so it was just a quick review," Hollis said.

"We're baking sandies," Cooper said. "Uncle Hollis, can you stay for dinner?"

"Yeah, bud, stay for dinner," Blake said, looking at him.

"I wish I could," Hollis groaned. "But I can't stay. I was actually on my way to New York and wanted to stop by for a little visit. I have to get back to catch my next flight"

"Aw, man," Cooper grumped.

"I promise I'll come back soon, buddy," Hollis said. "In the meantime, you take care of my little sister for me, okay? Don't let her get into any trouble. You know how she can be."

"Okay." Cooper giggled. "I'm pretty sure she keeps me out of trouble and Dad too."

"Good," Hollis said with a wink, turning to me. "And you take care of my friends. I will see you soon, okay? I love you."

"I love you too," I said, hugging him tightly and smiling as he kissed me on the cheek.

"It was good to see you, man," Blake said, shaking his hand.

Blake and Hollis walked out of the kitchen and to the front door. Cooper and I went back to baking the cookies and talking about future recipes. Once I heard the front door shut, I let out a deep breath and shook my head, thankful Hollis didn't figure anything out. If he did, I wasn't really sure who he would be angrier at, me or Blake. I was pretty sure he would have Blake's head on a stick if he knew what was going on. He still had that mentality that his baby sister could do no wrong. It was cute but annoying at the same time.

It wasn't that I was ashamed of what Blake and I had, but it was a mixture of things. For one, I didn't even know what exactly we did have, and two, my brother and family would never be able to understand what we saw in each other. While the age difference didn't bother me at all, it would bother my family, my mother especially. And lastly, and definitely most importantly, we didn't want Cooper to know what was happening. We didn't even understand fully what was between us, and the last thing Cooper needed was to have high hopes about me being in his life for a very long time. If things went awry or Blake ran in the other direction again, it would be impossible to help Cooper understand that. He was just a kid, and he'd been in an adult world for far too long already.

I put the thoughts out of mind and accepted the happiness of seeing my brother, if only for a few hours. Cooper and I went to work getting the cookies baked, plating them, cleaning up the kitchen, and then moving on through the day. He had a ton of energy that day, so all three of us tossed a baseball around in the backyard. I was really impressed on how Blake handled Cooper and gently tried to teach him things, not getting upset when he wasn't very good at it. When we were done, it was nearly dinnertime, so I whipped up some spaghetti because it was easy, and we all ate in the living room, watching a movie.

The day was long, and I was exhausted from the emotional upheaval as well as the physical one. By the time I was done with the dishes, I was ready for bed. I smiled at Cooper and Blake in the living room, talking about Hogwarts and what house his dad would be in. I walked around the corner and up the stairs to the bedroom, leaving Cooper and Blake to fend for themselves. I figured it was time they started doing things just the two of them. It was important for Cooper to see his dad still loved him. And on top of that, I didn't have much left in me.

I walked into my room and let out a deep breath, staring over at my comfy bed. I couldn't wait to get inside of it and pull the covers up over my head. I undressed and changed into a pair of pajamas and brushed my teeth and hair. When I was done and about to click off the light, there was a knock on the door. I opened it to find Blake standing there looking slightly worried.

"I wanted to come check on you," he said. "You just disappeared."

"I know." I smiled. "I'm sorry. I'm so exhausted. I feel like I could sleep for a year. I think with my brother and everything else, my body just needs some rest."

"I completely understand." He smiled in relief. "I wanted to make sure nothing's happened."

"Nothing has happened," I replied.

"All right, then. I'll leave you to your rest," he said, stepping forward and wrapping his arms around my waist. "But before I do, I'll leave you with a bit of my thoughts."

He grinned as he leaned in and pressed his lips against mine, giving me a deep searing kiss. His tongue moved through my mouth, and he pulled me even closer to him. By the time he pulled away, I was breathing heavily, my head slightly dizzy. He set me down carefully and backed back into the hallway.

"Sweet dreams," he whispered with a wink.

I stood in the doorway watching as he walked down and into his room. I shook my head, feeling the aftereffects that man left with me. For the first time, I really hated that he and I had to be a secret.

Chapter 25

Blake

I finished up at work and jumped in my car, excited to get home and see Aly. She had been acting strange ever since Hollis had come, and I had to admit, it worried me a little bit. I was sure he didn't know about us, but maybe that was the issue. I knew they had a close family, and it was hard for her to keep secrets from them. Still, it was the best option at that moment in time. I had no idea where things were going between Aly and me, and I knew Hollis would think negatively about it. I could punch Hollis, though, for messing up a really good thing, even if he didn't know it was happening.

Things were looking up for the evening since Cooper had a lock-in sleepover thing at his school that night. I was looking forward to being alone with Aly again. Hopefully, she was feeling the same way about me. Pleasuring her had become my new obsession, and I spent my nights alone thinking of all the ways I could make her quiver. I wanted to make her scream. I wanted to hear that voice echoing through the house and not have to worry about waking up Cooper. I wanted to let loose and have her do the same. She was tense the last time, even though it was amazing, and I knew if she could have let go, she would have enjoyed herself even more than she already had. There was something about the way her voice sounded when she was in ecstasy. It was freeing.

I pulled up at the house and parked in the driveway, obviously not wanting to see my son go but ready for some alone time. When I got inside, the house was pretty quiet, and I figured Aly was helping him get ready for the night. I hung up my coat and went to my room to change my clothes. There was a pile of my clean laundry on the bed, and I smiled, thinking about Aly singing along to her music, dancing through the house with stacks of clean clothes. She took such good care of us and I was so grateful for her playful demeanor while she did it.

When I was done changing, I headed down to the living room and found Cooper sitting at the table with his bookbag packed with fun stuff for his sleepover. He looked up at me and smiled as I walked in, getting up and hugging me tightly. Aly walked out of the kitchen with snacks in her hand packed neatly in a Ziploc bag.

"Hey." She smiled. "We were just getting ready to get Cooper to his sleepover."

"It's gonna be so cool, Dad," he said. "They made the gym into a beanbag movie theater, and we have camping tents set up all around to sleep in."

"That sounds like a blast," I said, ruffling his hair. "We're really going to miss you."

"I know. I was worried about that," he said seriously. "So, I left some ice cream for you guys in the fridge and put out the Harry Potter series. It's okay, Dad. I won't be gone too long."

I held back a laugh, marveling at how grown up he was sounding. I hugged him tightly and glanced up at Aly who was standing watching with her hand over her mouth. I stood up and stretched, smiling big at how sweet my son was.

"All right, buddy. I'll drive you over," I said.

Cooper hugged Aly, and we headed off to his school. I pulled up out front and handed him his bag. The teacher walked out and waved, ready to lead him inside. Other kids were arriving, too, and Cooper was already lost in the excitement.

"Call if you need anything," he said.

"I will," Cooper replied opening the door. "I love you Dad."

I shook my head as I headed off, glad to see he was doing so well. I sped back to the house to see Aly, excitement bubbling up in my stomach. When I got back, I found her in her room, staring at the computer. I walked over and without saying a word, grabbed her by the hand and led her down the hall to my bedroom. Once inside, I picked her up and tossed her on the bed, watching as she bounced up and down giggling.

Instantly, relief flooded through me, watching her smile and laugh, obviously into what was happening. For a minute, I had thought maybe she was done with me, but it was obviously not the case. I walked over to the nightstand and opened the drawer, grabbing a handful of condoms and tossing them on the bed next to her with a grin. Her eyes opened wide, and she pulled her lips together, obviously not expecting that reaction from me. Immediately, I started to strip, taking off my shirt and looking down at her.

"Take off your clothes," I ordered.

She smiled and took off all her clothes and laid back, watching me toss my boxers in the hamper. I slowly climbed across the bed until I was over her and leaned down, kissing her lips softly. I pulled back and looked deeply into her eyes, feeling her legs moving up my sides.

"I want to hear you scream my name," I whispered.

I grabbed her hands and pulled them over her head, locking them down with mine. I kissed her hard and fast, dominating her body. She immediately submitted, letting me do and say whatever I wanted. I could tell she liked the way I took control. Slowly, I moved my face down hers, kissing her neck and listening to her breath begin to quicken. She gripped tightly to my hands with hers, rubbing her soft smooth leg up and down my side. I loved how it felt pressing my body against hers, how I could feel every inch of her wanting me, craving me. She whimpered softly in my ear as I nibbled at her earlobe, starting out soft and dropping one of my hands down to her breast. I squeezed her tit, running her nipple through my fingers until it stiffened in my hand.

I slowly sat up on my knees and looked down at her, taking her legs and putting them up over my shoulders. I reached back and grabbed a condom, unwrapping it and sliding it down over my shaft. I rubbed her hot wet mound with my hand and warmed her up for what was to come. Slowly, I maneuvered my cock at her entrance, rubbing up and down through her juices. She gasped as I pushed forward, entering her slowly, down to the base of my shaft.

"Give me your hand," I said, taking it and pushing it down over her clit. "Rub your pussy while I fuck you like this."

She bit her lip and nodded, watching as I gripped her thighs and began to push and pull, my cock diving deep inside of her. She moaned loudly, her fingers dancing over her nub, rubbing it at the pace at which I thrust my hips. I bit my lip and closed my eyes, drowning in how tight and wet she was wrapped around my cock, her voice starting to get louder and louder. I reached down and pulled her lips apart, rubbing my hand over hers as she pleasured herself. She tilted her head back and rolled her eyes, lifting her shoulders from the bed. She began to pant wildly as I thrust fast and hard inside of her. She was reaching her climax, but I knew it wouldn't be the only one that night.

I took my hand from hers and pounded into her, the sound of my body slapping against hers echoing through the room. She arched her chest in the air as she exploded into an orgasm, her pussy clamping hard around my cock. I didn't slow down. I kept pushing harder and faster until she finally collapsed back on the bed. She pulled her hand away as I moved her legs from my shoulders and bent them at the knee. I pushed them wide open and looked down at her.

She pushed her hips up and widened her legs, giving me ample room to thrust as fast and hard as I could. My body slapped over and over again against her clit, and she reached up, rubbing her fingernails down my chest. She moaned, pulling her legs farther apart, grabbing her knees for stability. She wailed loudly, matching her moans with my speed. I growled, loving the way it sounded, loving to hear her in ecstasy. She was so wet, my cock slipped out several times, but I grabbed it and rammed back into her again, each time making her gasp.

I leaned forward and slowed my pace, pushing deep inside her. She groaned, grabbing my shoulders and pulling me into her. I reached above her and grabbed several pillows before sitting up on my knees.

"Lift up." I smiled.

She smirked and lifted her ass in the air, while I strategically placed the pillows beneath her. Once stable, she lowered back down and spread her legs wide, running her fingers down through her juices. I smiled, grabbing my cock and moving forward, slowly gliding it inside of her. Her eyes went wide, and she screamed out in pleasure, grabbing her bouncing tits.

I smiled and grabbed her by the waist, starting out slow, pushing all the way in and then pulling almost all the way out. Ecstasy rolled through her expression as I fucked her at this new angle. She reached down and rubbed her clit, breathing heavily. I rolled my hips against her body, pushing my cock into the right place. She screamed out in ecstasy, reaching up and grabbing the headboard. Within seconds, she was stiffening again, calling my name over and over. She rubbed her clit fast and hard and then exploded right in front of me. Even through the condom, the rush of her hot juices burst around my cock.

I immediately grabbed onto her and grunted as I thrust deep, pushing her body forward. I did it over and over until finally, I released. I groaned, letting out a long breath as my seed erupted from my cock, sending waves of pleasure bolting through my entire body. As the last of it moved away, I shivered, smiling down at her. I pulled out and rose from the bed, going to the bathroom to clean up.

By the time I came back, she was curled up in a ball, her eyes barely open. I smiled and climbed in next to her, putting my arm under her head and kissing her forehead. She smiled and closed her eyes, rolling to the side and draping her leg across me. Almost instantly, she was asleep, breathing so heavily, she was almost snoring. I chuckled and pulled her in closer, liking the way it felt to have her next to me in the bed. I looked up at the ceiling and sighed. I was liking it a bit more than I probably should.

Chapter 26

Aly

I woke up that Thursday morning feeling sick to my stomach. It wasn't anything drastic, but it definitely took me a minute to get out of bed. All my energy was drained even though I'd gone to bed early and slept nearly nine hours. I really hoped I wasn't coming down with something. I went through the day slowly, getting Cooper ready but doing the minimum I had to do. By the time Cooper went to bed that night, I was crashing in mine, not even telling anyone good night.

My alarm went off blaring in my ear, and I reached over, slapping the button hard. I rolled over on my side and rubbed my stomach, feeling that same queasiness only with more intensity. Slowly, I pulled myself out of bed and stood in front of the dresser, getting clothes out for the day. Before I could fully get the rest of the clothes out, I raced into the bathroom and threw up in the toilet. I sat back on my heels and closed my eyes, breathing heavily, wiping the sweat from my forehead. I felt terrible, dizzy, tired, and my stomach was doing flip-flops. I hadn't even eaten anything really the day before because I didn't have much of an appetite at all. It wasn't abnormal for me to get so caught up in work that I forgot to eat, so I hadn't really thought about it until I was dry heaving over the toilet.

I picked myself up and walked over to the sink, starting the cool water and splashing it on my face. I brushed my teeth and rinsed out my mouth. thinking about what could have possibly made me that ill. There was always the possibility that Cooper brought something home from school, but he wasn't sick at all. In fact, his appetite had increased. I opened the drawer out of habit and pulled out my birth control. I popped out the pill and tossed it back, stopping as I swallowed with a curiosity building in my mind. I walked back in the room and opened the calendar on my phone and started counting days. I must have counted at least ten times before realizing I hadn't gotten my period since I'd been there. I stood back and shook my head, not understanding how I could have possibly missed that.

I looked at the time and raced back into the bathroom and threw on my clothes. I had to get Cooper breakfast and get him off to school. The entire time I cooked, though, my mind was on that calendar, and my heart was fluttering wildly in my chest. I sat with him while he ate like normal and tried to pretend like there was nothing wrong with me. I had never had a pregnancy scare before and having to function and not being able to say anything about it was more difficult than I thought it would be.

After breakfast, we headed out to school, and I wished him a good day in class like I always did. Once he was out of sight, though, I tuned the GPS to the closest drug store and headed over to buy a pregnancy test—or four. I stood in the aisle staring at all the different options, unsure of which to try. I ended up buying the name brand ones, too afraid to leave it up to a store brand. I was shaking all the way back to the house, and I was glad I'd brought my big purse, so I could shove the tests in there in case Blake was up when I got home.

When I got there, I walked upstairs and shut and locked my bedroom door. I couldn't stop thinking about it. The only time we could have gotten pregnant would have been that first time, and it would be my luck that it happened. I started to beat myself up for not keeping up on my pills, for having unprotected sex, and even for getting involved with Blake at all. I took the tests into the bathroom but set them on the counter, unrolling the instructions and reading them very carefully.

I sighed and stood up, taking two of the tests from the packages and holding them up in front of me. I might as well take two and make myself feel better about whatever results they showed. I sat down on the toilet and peed on both of them, putting on the caps and setting them on the counter. I cleaned myself up and moved over to the bathtub where I sat staring down at the timer on my phone. When it finally dinged, I stood up and breathed deeply, gathering my courage before walking over and staring down at them.

I'd made sure to get the digital ones so there would be no confusion over lines. Sure, enough, both of them read "pregnant". I put my hand on the counter and steadied myself, feeling my knees going weak. I took the tests and put them in my drawer, shoving the bag with the boxes in my trash can. Slowly, I walked out to the bedroom and sat down on the edge of the bed, staring into space. I wanted to cry, just let go and completely bawl my eyes out. This wasn't in the plans. Blake already had a son, and after everything he'd been through, I couldn't imagine him chomping at the bit to have another child. We barely knew each other, despite living together for the last month.

It was supposed to be fun, passionate; a good time while I was here. This was not supposed to be something that lasted a lifetime. And what about school? I wasn't finished yet, had no real career, and struggled enough working and keeping up with classes much less having a baby to contend with as well. My whole life I had been the most careful person in the world and not just with sex but with everything. The one time I chose to throw caution to the wind and have some torrid love affair with my lifelong crush, I ended up getting myself knocked up.

I didn't know what to do. I couldn't call my mom or my sisters; they would lose their absolute fucking minds. I looked back up at the bathroom and walked quickly in there, reopening the drawer and pulling the tests out. I couldn't hide them there. I didn't want there to be any chance Blake or Cooper came across them. So, I took them to my closet, found my suitcase, and zipped them into the inner compartment. I ran back and grabbed the boxes, too, and did the same thing. I felt like I was covering up a murder. I loved kids. I really thought that when the time came though, that I would be shouting it from the rooftops with a loving husband, not sitting alone in a dimly lit room, completely across the country from my family, hiding the evidence.

I had to tell Blake. Of course, I did, but I had no idea how to do that. It wasn't something I could bring up at the dinner table and making it a surprise was not in the cards. I sighed and went back over to my computer. I needed to put it out of my mind by getting some schoolwork done. That posed a much more difficult task than I first thought. My mind kept bouncing back to the tests, and I still felt sick as a dog and wanted to take a nap every five seconds.

I suffered my way through the rest of the day, mainly holed up in my room except when I had to go down and try to get some food in my stomach. I didn't want to run into Blake, not yet. I wanted to have time to think about what I was going to say to him. I hoped he didn't think I'd done it on purpose, because I was definitely not that kind of person. We were both at fault for what happened in the laundry room, and though I should have stood up and said stop, I didn't.

When Cooper was home from school, I did my best to be present and pay attention, but all I could focus on was the damn pregnancy tests. Luckily, after he finished his homework, all he wanted to do was play video games. It gave me the time to cook dinner and think about things some more. I needed to not wait to tell Blake. I needed to rip the Band-Aid off right away. It would only get worse as time passed, and the last thing I wanted was a complete emotional breakdown in front of the man. I was still pretty numb from finding out, as it was, so it might be easier before the hormones kicked in and the emotions took control.

All throughout dinner, I was worried about what Blake was going to say. I sat quietly, trying to act like I was paying attention, eating my macaroni and cheese. Blake glanced over at me several times, catching me staring off into space, and I cleared my throat, sitting up in the chair and smiling. Finally, when he came back into the room after putting Cooper to bed, I completely chickened out. I didn't know what to say or do, so I sat on the couch silently. Blake raised an eyebrow at me and walked over, putting his hand out.

"You okay?" he asked as he scooped me up into his arms.

"Yeah," I said, leaning back. "Just a little tired, that's all. I haven't really been feeling too hot lately."

"Come on," he said with a pouty lip. "Let's go to bed then."

I nodded, kicking myself for not telling him. Instead, I took his hand and followed him back to his bed. I needed him, especially then, and it was starting to feel like an addiction more than anything.

Chapter 27

Blake

We had really great sex that night, though I had to admit it was a bit gentler than normal. Aly seemed to be in that mood, like she needed me to have my arms around her, be close, take our time with things. Afterward, we lay in bed talking, our hands intertwined, laughing about silly things that happened during the day, about business, and about life in general. We usually always had great conversations when it was the two of us. There wasn't anything stressful in our lives, and it was a time both of us could take off the nanny and Dad hats and say whatever we were thinking about at the time. I really loved how we got along so well. It was refreshing.

"I'm pretty sure my assistant, Inez, thinks I'm a nutcase by now." I chuckled.

"Why?" Aly asked.

"Because over the last year, I've been on an emotional roller coaster, and just in the last two months, it's been up, down, up, down," I said. "I'm pretty sure she keeps mace in her drawer, thinking one day I'm going to snap."

"Oh." She chuckled. "I'm sure she understands. She's been with you a long time, right?"

"Since I started the company," I said.

"Then, she should know by now that you aren't going to go postal on anyone," she said.

"So, what do you want in the future?" I asked Aly. "I know you're going to school, but I don't know what for."

"I'm going to school for early childhood development," she said after a brief look I couldn't name flashed across her face. "When I'm done with that, I'm thinking probably teaching or something along those lines."

"How about you?" she asked. "I mean, I know you have your career, but do you imagine yourself having more kids or getting married again ever?"

"Kids?" I chuckled. "No. I'm too old for that now. I can't imagine starting over with a baby. And getting married again? I don't know. I don't know that I want to ever risk hurting that badly ever again. "

Aly got quiet, and I squeezed her close to me, reaching over and shutting off the light. I figured she had a long day and was probably exhausted. I scooted down in the bed and held her close as I fell asleep with her in my arms. I always slept so well with her right there, and even though it was kind of frightening to have that revelation, I held her close anyway.

The next day at work, I pumped through some big projects that were on the books and cleared out my inbox all by lunchtime. Inez went out and grabbed us takeout, and I sat at my desk, eating my sub, thinking about my life. Everything was so different now. Life was getting better day by day, and I could see it reflecting in everything I did, from getting up in the morning to not chewing anyone's head off before coffee and being productive and being there for Cooper. It hadn't been this good in a really long time, and I had Aly to thank for that. Everything good that had come into my life had done so since her arrival.

She had blown into our lives with the motivation and fortitude to make things better on all ends of the spectrum. She didn't take no for an answer, and she let me know when things weren't right, and I needed that, even if I'd pushed it away in the beginning. It was always hard for me to take criticism, especially when it came to my child or the way I lived my life, but she didn't care. She made sure I stuck to my duties as a father and pulled my ass up out of the mud so I could keep the beautiful life I'd built, even if it had been at someone else's side.

Cooper and I were getting along better than we ever had before. When Aly first got there, we barely said two words to each other, and come to find out, my son thought I didn't like him because he couldn't throw a baseball or play football. I didn't care about any of those things, but I didn't even notice he felt that way until Aly gave him a voice. I had a child in my home, and I'd treated him like a stranger. It wasn't how I wanted to be as a father, and I think she could see that somewhere in my eyes. When Aly told me I needed to get to know my son better, I was pissed, but that anger drove me to never have that happen again. It pushed me to listen to my son and find out what he really thought. By doing that, we created a bond I hoped would never be broken.

From all those positive changes at home, came a more responsible and stronger self. I went to work and opened my eyes for the first time in an entire year. I realized I wasn't doing my job. I was putting everything on the shoulders of my assistant, and that wasn't fair. I expected to stay where I was but didn't want to lift a finger to do anything. I was drowning in my own depression like there was a weight pulling me down. After Aly came, I really started to snap out of it. I started to be more energized at work, and my work ethic had been completely dusted off. For the first time in a year, I was making money again instead of coasting through, hoping it would take care of itself.

It felt great to be back. It felt good to wake up every morning and smile at the sunshine instead of closing the blinds and going back to sleep. That pertained to life too. It felt good to not close the blinds on life anymore as well. Going to the gym had become something I did to stay in shape, no longer something I did to make myself feel better or to release whatever anger and frustration were going on in my head at the moment. I did things because I wanted to, not because I felt obligated. All of that started the moment Aly had told me to let go of my anger. She had enabled me to recognize what I was doing to my family and to myself by holding onto the past and all the emotion that was involved in that.

When my wife died, there was so much to think about, so much to work through. I was heartbroken, angry, and sad that she'd died, leaving our son without his mother. All those emotions were swirling around inside of me, and they were so strong and overwhelming that I had to shut them out instead of facing them head-on. I had finally reached a point where it was possible for me to let it go, to want to move on, and let the past lie. Sure, I didn't always let go of my anger completely. There were times when I was angry for no reason, but those times were fewer and farther between, and I stopped letting it rule my life. It was like a million-pound weight lifted off my shoulders.

By the end of the day, I had really knocked out most everything I needed to get done. Usually by that point, I was still trying to catch up on the week before. I left the office feeling good, with a bright attitude, ready to go home and snuggle up with Aly for the night. When I pulled up to the house, I noticed the lights in the house were on. By this time, most of them were usually off. I parked the car and went inside, turning the corner to find Cooper sitting at the kitchen table. He was usually in bed by now, even on a Friday night. I had stayed late at work to make sure I didn't need to do anything this weekend, so I knew something was up.

"Hey, buddy," I said, hanging my coat over the back of the chair and putting my suitcase on the counter. "You should be in bed by now. Where's Aly?"

"Aly's really sick," he said. "She tried to take care of me anyway, but she couldn't get off of the bathroom floor. I told her it was okay, and I would wait for you. I didn't want to go to bed until you came home to check on her."

"Aw, buddy," I said, hugging him. "That's really sweet of you. I'll walk upstairs with you, and you go ahead and climb in bed. I'll go check on Aly and make sure she's okay."

He nodded and stood up, following me down the hall and up the stairs. I smiled down on him, dropping a kiss to his forehead as I covered him up and wished him sweet dreams. I shut the door behind me and raced to Aly's room. I was really worried from the moment I got home and saw Cooper sitting at the table by himself, but I didn't want to panic and scare him. I made my way to her bedroom and walked in carefully, calling her name.

"Aly?" I said, walking toward the bathroom.

"In here," she groaned.

I turned the corner and found her sitting on the floor in front of the toilet, her head leaning against the wall, her face as white as a ghost. I bent down in front of her and felt her forehead. She felt a little warm but nothing too crazy. She pushed herself upright and shook her head.

"What's going on?" I asked kindly. "Are you okay?"

"Yeah," she said. "I must have eaten something bad. I will be okay. I need to rest, that's all."

"Okay," I said. "Come on. Let's get you up and into bed."

She reached her arm up, and I helped her to her feet. As soon as I saw she was having trouble with balance, I scooped her up into my arms and carried her to the bed. I tucked her in and kissed her on the forehead, watching as she quickly fell asleep. I wanted to help, but I knew there was nothing I could do but let her rest.

Chapter 28

Aly

I hated lying. I always had, even when I was a kid and I knew telling the truth would get me in trouble. I was probably honest to a fault at times, but it was important to me. With this, though, I couldn't tell Blake, not after the conversation we had. No matter how much it bothered me to lie to him – and it bothered me to the point of tears – the news would not be happy news to him. He might even explode on me, feeling backed into a corner when all we were supposed to be doing was having a good time. He'd told me point blank that having a baby was the last thing in the world he wanted. Yes, that question was posed in a manner in which we were thinking about the future and not in a position where he really thought I was pregnant, but still, that was how he felt deep down inside.

Now, I was at a point where I had to figure out how to get out of his employ before I started showing. I wanted to figure out everything on my own and then decide when the right time to tell him was. I couldn't take another bad night, another bad word, and I couldn't deal with the trauma that went along with telling a man who didn't want any more children that I was pregnant with his baby. I needed to try to stay calm and keep myself together, I had bigger responsibilities now and this child had to be my first priority.

I wish I could say that it was just an inconvenience, that him not wanting me or the baby didn't bother me, but that was extremely far from the truth. It hurt my heart more than a lot, and I already felt like he'd kicked me out of his life, just by thinking about the choices I had to make. I had fallen for him, and I hadn't even seen it coming. I'd told myself over and over again that it was nothing more than two people having really great sex, but that was a bunch of bullshit. I had fallen in love with the man, looked forward to seeing him, loved hearing his voice, and wanted to be around him as much as I could be.

On top of that, from the first moment I'd met Cooper, we'd bonded. I loved that little boy and already couldn't imagine going a day without having him in my life. I'd started out by investing myself in the job, but it had turned into me investing my heart into both Blake and Cooper. Now, it was breaking very quickly. I hadn't ever had a heartbreak that felt like this, but there I was, just wanting to get out and get away before it got any worse. I knew, though, with a child that was Blake's, I was going to continue to feel that heartbreak for a very long time, especially after I told him about the baby.

I still couldn't believe his child was growing in my belly, making me as sick as I had gotten. I needed to see a doctor, but at this point, it would give me away. I needed to go home, be with my family, and figure it all out from there. I woke up that Saturday morning completely unable to focus, barely able to get around, and feeling miserable about the situation. I was also sicker than I'd ever been before in my life..

Originally, I was going to try to get through the day, make some toast, try to eat that, and coast through. It was Saturday, so I didn't have to take Cooper anywhere, and there wasn't really any housework that desperately needed to get done. However, after getting up and barely making it down to the kitchen for some bread and water, I knew there was no way I was going to get it done.

"What are you doing out of bed?" Blake asked, rounding the corner. "You still look like you feel terrible."

"I do," I said, shaking my head. "I thought if I got up and around, it would help me feel better, but it didn't. Do you mind if I take the day off?"

"Of course, you can, and it's technically your day off anyway, even though you never seem to take them."

"It doesn't feel like work when I'm hanging out with you," I smiled, grabbing onto the back of the chair. "I feel dizzy."

"I would imagine so," Blake said, picking me up in his arms. "You are probably dehydrated and need to get some food in your stomach. How about this? I will take you up, get you all tucked in, and Cooper and I will play nurse today."

"No, you guys should go have fun. It's a beautiful Saturday," I protested.

"Nope, it's already done. You always take such great care of us, today it's our turn," he said, carrying me up the stairs. "All I want you to do is sit back, relax, get hydrated, and let me know if there's anything at all that you need."

"Ok, but only because I don't have the energy to fight you on it," I acquiesced.

"I know," he said. "That's what I figured."

He carried me back up to my room and tucked me in bed. I laid my head on the pillow and stared up at the ceiling. I lay like that for quite a while, falling in and out of sleep, waking up, drinking some water, and then doing it all over again. A couple of hours later, I could hear the guys making their way up the stairs. It sounded like Blake was struggling, and Cooper was barking out orders. I pulled my eyebrows together and sat up in the bed, leaning back against the headboard. Around the corner both of them came, Blake balancing a TV on his knee as he tried to carry it without tripping over the cord, and Cooper behind him with a tray of soup and crackers.

I looked at them like they were crazy and then smiled at Cooper as he set the tray over my lap. I ruffled his hair and winked, both of us turning to Blake and watching as he struggled to get the television up on the stand in my room. He plugged it in and tossed me the remote, putting one finger up and disappearing around the corner. When he came back, he had a cable box and universal remote. He hooked it up in my room and smiled, proud of himself for a job well done.

"We thought you should drink some soup." Cooper smiled.

"And watch really crappy movies while you were shacked up in bed," Blake said.

"Thanks," I chuckled, trying to be grateful.

"And this is chicken noodle. It always makes me feel better," Cooper said. "We got it from this restaurant that my dad really likes."

"Oh, that sounds so special." I smiled. "Thank you so much."

"You're welcome," he said happily. "When I was a little boy—"

"Yeah, because you're so grown now." Blake laughed.

"I am," Cooper grumbled. "Anyway, when I was a little boy, my mom would feed me soup when I was sick, and every time, I would magically get better."

"Moms have a way of doing that, don't they?" I smiled.

The fact that Cooper was so excited about making me feel better was actually making me feel even worse about lying to them. I felt so guilty, like such a complete asshole, but what was I supposed to do? Tell them this illness wouldn't be over for nine months? Cooper wouldn't get it, and Blake would lose his mind over it, so I was really stuck between a rock and a hard place. They were going to continue to play nursemaid until I either came clean or faked like I was feeling better. I really only had one choice there, but for today, I wasn't planning on getting out of bed. Blake had totally misread what I was looking for in a day off.

I needed a break, and not only a break from work, but a break from him, from Cooper, even though he made me smile, and a complete break from life. I needed to be able to lie there in silence, trying to reach the point where I could make sense of everything going on. I needed to think about where I wanted to go from there and how I wanted to break the news to Blake. I didn't want two people rushing around me, trying to make me feel better with no clue as to what was going on in the first place.

Irritation startled to settle in when they both took a seat in the chairs in the room. I just wanted to be alone, dammit. Why couldn't Blake see that? I really wanted to tell them to get out and leave me the hell alone, but I couldn't do that. Especially not to the sweet little boy who just wanted to make me feel better. Instead, I would have to deal with it and hope I drifted off to sleep instead of being subjected to another round of Indiana Jones marathons.

I lay in the bed not saying much, dozing off and waking back up to find Cooper asleep in the chair and Blake completely enthralled in whatever movie was on the television. Finally, when the sun had gone down, and we had all eaten dinner in my room, Cooper and Blake decided it was time for bed. Cooper walked over to me and laid his head on my chest.

"I hope you feel better, Aly," he said. "I hope my magic nurse skills cured you."

"Aw, you did make me feel better, thank you," I said, hugging him back and trying to force down the lump in my throat.

"Come on, bud," Blake said, standing at the door.

As they walked out, he winked at me and shut the door behind him. I sighed and laid back in the bed, grabbing the remote and turning off the television. It had been the most stressful day of rest I'd ever been subjected to. I turned over on my side and thought about Blake and how much I cared about him. In any other situation, what they'd done for me that day would have been one of the sweetest things ever, but under the circumstances, it was confusing and even more heartbreaking. Every time my hormones would flare up, I felt like either crying or screaming, and that was definitely not a symptom of the stomach flu.

What needed to happen to push me into telling Blake was I needed to make a pact with myself. I would not sleep with him again until I told him I was pregnant. I had to be honest after all these lies and continuing to sleep with him would only make my heartbreak that much worse.

Chapter 29

Blake

Normally, I hated Mondays like I hated peas, but for some reason, this particular Monday wasn't bad at all. I went in with a positive attitude, went straight to work, and plowed through it. I had clients calling, partners calling, and a really important conference call with the head of the NFL that day. All of which went off without a hitch, and we were again an official sponsor of the league. The company was coming right back to where it was before I had fallen completely apart. We were on an upswing, and I was amazed at how much being back at the helm really helped. People wanted to hear my voice. They wanted to know I was in control of the company and in control of myself.

When Inez came in with a message, she no longer talked and looked at me with a sense of pity. Instead, she looked at me like she used to, with respect and admiration. It was something that really warmed my heart and reminded me how lucky I had found myself in life. Near the end of the day, I remembered that I wanted to do something big for Inez to thank her for everything she'd done for the company while I was incapable. So, I wrote her a check for a hundred thousand dollars, roughly the amount she should have gotten paid on top of her current salary and dropped it on her desk in an envelope on my way out of the office.

It would be a huge surprise, and I wasn't much of one to accept thanks for something that I should be thanking her for. I left the office and hopped in my Mercedes, pulling my phone from my hip as it buzzed. It was a text from Inez.

This better not be payment to dispose of a body, she texted.

Nope, it's a thank-you gift for keeping us from going under while I went under for the last year, I texted back, laughing.

Well, I know you don't like thank-yous so I'll just say it's about damn time you recognized, she texted back with a smiley face.

I threw my head back and laughed loudly, tossing my phone into the passenger seat and heading for home. When I got there, I whistled as I made my way up to the porch. As soon as I opened the front door, the smell food cooking in the kitchen wrapped around me. It smelled delicious and created a warm feeling in the house. I walked back to find Aly and Cooper at the counter. I stood in the doorway of the kitchen and smiled, watching Cooper standing on a chair, stirring a large pot of stew, while Aly cut up vegetables.

"Whatever that is, it smells amazing," I said.

"It's stew," Cooper chirped. "Because it's cold outside."

"Well, that's perfect," I said, walking in. "It's supposed to snow tonight for the first time this season."

"Really?" Cooper said with excitement. "Yay!"

I sat down at the table and grabbed an apple, biting into it and smiling as I watched them cook. Everything was the picture of perfection. There was hot food on the stove, the house smelled amazing, everyone was laughing and talking, and the mood was light. In the past, this would have totally freaked me out like it did the time we all watched Harry Potter together, but right then, it didn't scare me at all. It was a good feeling to be normal again, to do normal things, to feel like a family. I didn't know how Aly felt about it, but I was content, and I hadn't been content in a very long time. With her, there was no race to the finish, no forcefulness to be together. We all kind of pulled toward each other, and everything else came naturally.

Maybe before, I was afraid to be happy, not afraid of commitment. Maybe I felt like wallowing in my own self-pity was what I was supposed to do when I became a widower. Either way, I knew immediately as I sat there watching them goof around, that wallowing wasn't what I wanted at all. I wanted to be happy, smiling, and loved, not depressed, angry, and bitter. In fact, I didn't feel like I was involved enough in the happiness going on. I set my apple on the table and stood up, rolling up my sleeves. I was going to join in on this one.

"You mind if I cut up some of those potatoes and help out?" I asked Aly, smiling at her.

"Please," she said, handing me the knife. "By all means, chop away."

"Thank you," I said, grabbing a potato and beginning to cut.

"I didn't even think you knew how to use a knife," Cooper said, making us all laugh. "I thought pizza and Chinese were your limits."

"I see how you are." I laughed. "Calling me out like that. Okay, I got your number."

We all continued to laugh and joke until dinner was ready. Cooper and I set the table and then I walked over, helping Aly carry the big pot of stew over. We set it on the towel, and I stayed standing, serving our bowls and passing the home baked rolls Aly and Cooper had made. We sat and ate, and I couldn't believe how amazing the stew was.

"Cooper made the whole thing on his own." Aly smiled. "I just helped cut the veggies because it took less time that way, and we knew you would be home soon."

"That's perfect," I said.

After dinner, I let Cooper go off to play video games, and Aly and I cleared the table. In a way, I did it on purpose, wanting to have a moment of alone time with her. I cleared the plates in the trash and then wrapped up the leftovers as she started to rinse the dishes. She looked so happy standing there in her yoga pants and a T-shirt, and her skin was almost glowing. Instantly, I wanted to put my hands on her. I wanted to pull her close and not let her go. I knew it couldn't be something that happened right then with Cooper in the other room, but I wanted to let her know what I was thinking about.

I put the leftover stew in the fridge and wiped off my hands, walking up behind her. I leaned down and nipped at her ear, breathing heavily. She groaned softly and closed her eyes, leaning her head back and pushing her ass into my erection. I growled into her ear, wanting to take her right then and there, wanting to wrap her up and bend her over the dishes like I wanted to do before. I couldn't, though, not with Cooper sitting right in the other room. I had to try to behave myself as much as possible. It was really hard to do with the sound of her whispered moans in my ears. No matter how much I had of her, I always wanted more, and something as simple as her helping me clean up turned me on to the point to where I was ready to call it a day.

"Later on, when the house is quiet, I'm going to make you moan like you never have before," I whispered.

"Oh, yeah?" she whispered back. "And how are you going to do that?"

"I'm going to take you upstairs, lay you down, and lick your pussy from top to bottom," I whispered, grinding my cock into her ass. "Then when you come, I'm going to turn you over and fuck you from behind."

"Mmmm," she groaned.

My cock was so hard, it was throbbing in my pants and almost to the point of being painful. I breathed a heavy sigh and backed up, knowing I couldn't go any further. I hopped around the kitchen, trying to talk my erection down as Aly watched me, laughing hysterically. I walked over and gave her a big kiss and smiled before walking out of the kitchen and into the living room where Cooper was.

"Hey, bud," I said, sitting down next to him. "Whatcha playing?"

"Halo," he said, his eyes glued to the screen.

"I like that game," I said.

"You want to play with me?" he asked. "It'll do split screen."

"Yeah," I said. "Hook me up."

From there on out for the next few hours, Cooper and I were glued to the television screen. I didn't really care for video games at all, but I loved doing things with Cooper that made him happy. He was in heaven having me there playing his Xbox with him, and that made it all worthwhile to me. Aly came in and out of the room, bringing us sodas, snacks, and anything else we might need. She looked at me and winked when she walked back out of the room, obviously ecstatic that Cooper and I were getting along so well. It was amazing to me how much she cared about my and Cooper's relationship. It was completely selfless, yet she made it the center of her world. She was an amazing woman. I'd known that from the beginning, but I was just starting to appreciate it.

"All right, bud," I said after about two hours. "Let's go up to your room and read some together. Then it's time for bed."

"Okay," he sighed, turning off the console and putting up the controllers. "I'm starting the new Fantastic Beasts series. It's the next adventure in the Wizarding World."

"Awesome, let's do this, tell Aly good night," I said, smiling over at her.

"Night," he said, running over and giving her a hug.

"Night, buddy, I'll see you in the morning," she replied.

We went upstairs, and he changed into his pajamas before climbing into bed and handing me the book. He loved it when I read to him. He said it made him feel like he was part of the story instead of reading it from the outside. I missed feeling the magic of being a child like that, but I was glad that even after everything that had happened, he still hadn't lost it.

I read two chapters to him and then carefully closed the book, finding him falling asleep during the last page. I smiled and pulled the blanket up as he snored, turning over and cuddling into his pillow. I chuckled as I turned off the light and quietly shut the door. I walked back downstairs and found Aly lounging on the couch in the living room reading a book. She looked up and marked her page before smiling and closing it. I stood for a minute just staring at her and smiling.

"What?" she asked, blushing.

"Nothing. You're so pretty, that's all," I said.

"You're ridiculous." She laughed, standing up.

"Ridiculous, huh?" I said, walking forward. "I'll show you ridiculous."

I rushed forward and grabbed her, picking her up and throwing her over my shoulder caveman style. She squealed and laughed, kicking her legs as I turned and hit the light switch. Up the stairs we went and down the hall to my bedroom where I stopped and threw her down on the bed, breathing heavy and pushing my laughter to the side. It was time to get serious.

Chapter 30

Aly

From the moment he nibbled on my ear in that kitchen, I'd lost my resolve. To make it even worse, when I walked in to find him hanging out with Cooper, playing video games and being a good dad, my panties pretty much had already melted off my body. The entire evening, I replayed the words he whispered to me in the kitchen, over and over in my head. Every single time, I got butterflies in my stomach, and I was soaking wet. I wanted that man all the time, and ever since my pregnancy symptoms had started, it was all I could think about. I hated myself a bit that it was so easy for me to cave in like this. I had promised not to sleep with him again until I told him about the baby, but by the time I was up in bed, it was definitely too late for that. It wasn't like I could stop and say, "Wait, hold on before you stick it in. I gotta tell you something."

Still, I had sworn it, and not out loud but to myself, that I had to be honest, that I had to tell him everything that was going on. I had to be the woman who stood for something. I had to be the mother to this baby that it deserved, and part of that was telling its father he was going to be a dad again. It was so much harder to do than it was to say in my head. Just getting the words to spew from my mouth was going to be an act of God, much less finding an alone time where we weren't ripping each other's clothes off. My body was craving him like a drug.

I sat up in the bed and took off my shirt and bra, lying back down to scoot my yoga pants off and toss them on the floor. He smiled and started to undress, biting his lip as I sat up on my knees and rubbed my tits with my palms. He chuckled and shook his head, trying to get his shoes untied. I laughed and scooted closer to him, quickly unbuttoning his shirt and sliding it back off his shoulders. I ran my hands down the front of him, his warm, soft skin under my fingertips. His body was perfect like it was sculpted by the gods. Every crease and curve flowed right into the other. His muscles bulged in his chest, and his six-pack ran right to the top of his pants. He laid down in the bed, and I undid his pants, pulling them down and off. I ran my fingers over the V of his abdomen, watching as it disappeared under his boxers.

Everything about the man was sexy, from the way he looked at me and the way he talked to me to the way he held that amazing body. I couldn't help wanting him all the time, and I was pretty sure there wasn't a woman on the planet who would be able to resist that charming, sexy smile, especially with how he would smirk and wink at me whenever no one was looking. I was working myself up so hard, I could barely keep my hands off him. I took a deep breath to calm down and then pulled his boxers down and off, staring at his huge cock bouncing back and forth.

I reached out and grabbed it in my hand, rubbing my palm up and down his shaft. He groaned and closed his eyes, pulling his arms up behind his head. I smiled and leaned forward, rubbing my lips across its mushroom tip. Slowly, I pushed my tongue from my mouth and swirled it around the head. He jerked slightly and gasped, making me smile. I opened my mouth and sheathed my teeth, sliding slowly down his dick until I was about three-quarters of the way down. I sucked hard as I twisted my head, bringing it back to the top and then going again, this time making my way all the way to the base.

I tightened my throat muscles and bobbed up and down for several seconds, his whole body tensing as I pulled my head back up his shaft. I didn't hesitate at the top, and I went straight back down, this time reaching up and cupping his balls in my hand. I rolled them around with the same speed that my tongue swirled through my mouth.

"Fuuuck," he groaned. "That feels fucking amazing."

I smiled with my mouth full and began to pick up the pace, my heading moving up and down, glancing up at him from time to time. He ran his hand through my hair, shaking his head, as I sucked him hard and fast. Finally, he reached up and grabbed my face, just as I was pulling the tip of his cock from my lips.

"Come here," he whispered. "Ride my cock."

I bit my bottom lip and smiled, pulling myself over him and scooting up to his dick. He reached over, grabbed a condom, and slid it on really fast. The whole time, I was thinking about how it was a waste of a rubber. When he was done, I hovered over his huge shaft and opened my legs, sliding down him with my warm, wet pussy. He groaned, throwing his head back and grabbing onto my waist tightly. First, I started by riding him slowly, moving up his shaft right to the tip and then sliding back down, swirling my hips at the bottom. As I went, though, I could feel the electricity shooting through me, and I found myself staying down, his cock deep inside, my body grinding against his.

I groaned loudly, swirling my hips faster and faster, my orgasm growing quickly. He grabbed onto my body and moved it around, helping me reach that climax. I put my hands down on his chest and wailed, bouncing up and down, feeling his shaft sliding in and out of my body. It was erotic, sensual, and oh god, I was about to come all over him. Just as the thought crossed my mind, he thrust his hips upward, and I exploded, my body shaking as I grabbed onto my tits and let him take control.

"Yes," he growled, feeling me clamp down on his cock.

As the waves of pleasure bolted through me, he lifted me about halfway up his shaft and held me there, pumping his hips fast and hard. His body connecting with mine increased the intensity of my orgasm, and then, I was like putty in his hands. When my orgasm had simmered, and I was able to function again, I shook my head, putting my fingers in my mouth and whining as he continued to pound into me harder and harder. He grabbed my waist and flipped me over on my back, grabbing his cock and immediately plunging into me hard and deep.

I opened my legs wide and bit back a scream, feeling him deeper inside of me. Normally by now, I would be winding down, but with the hormones blowing through me, all I could think about was getting nastier and dirtier. I looked up at him and smiled through my moan, bouncing up and down as he fucked me hard and fast.

"Yes," I called out, raising my hands over my head. "Fuck, yes!"

"Shhh." He laughed, putting his hand over my mouth.

I quieted, remembering we weren't the only ones in the house at that moment. He slowed his pace, leaning forward and wrapping my legs around his waist. He stopped moving for a moment and looked deeply into my eyes, making my heart skip a beat. Slowly, he lowered his head, pressing his lips gently against mine. The change of pace threw me off balance, but I liked it, I liked it a whole hell of a lot.

He ran his hand down my side and grabbed my thigh, keeping his lips firmly pressed against mine. I moaned into his mouth as he began to push deep inside of me, rubbing his body up mine. His other hand took my arm and pulled it up over my head, latching his fingers through mine as he lifted up, grinding his body down and into me. I had never felt anything change from that kind of lust to that kind of passion in such a short amount of time. It was like we went from fucking to making love in the blink of an eye, and I had to admit, my breath was completely taken away.

He looked deeply into my eyes as he moved forward and back, growling as his cock sank deeper inside of me. I pulled my hand free and rubbed it up his chest and over his cheek, watching as he hooked his arms under my knees and pushed them up toward my shoulders. I moaned, tilting my head back, feeling the intensity of the moment, my body heating faster and faster. As I came closer to yet another climax, he spread my knees apart and laid back into me, kissing me hard, pumping his hips fast and shallow. I moaned into his mouth as my body erupted, feeling his cock begin to pulse before he too blew open into orgasm. We laid there, feeling the pleasure roll through us, until all that was left were our mouths still connected.

He lifted his head up and wiped the hair out of my face, kissing me gently on the lips. I whimpered as he pulled out, completely blown away by what I'd just experienced. While he was in the bathroom, I got up and got dressed, knowing I couldn't sleep in there tonight. He came out and smiled at me, rubbing his hands down my arms.

"You going to your room?"

"Yeah, for tonight," I said, reaching up and kissing his cheek. "Thank you for that. It was amazing."

He smiled and swatted me on the butt as I made my way out of his room and quietly down the hall to mine. When I got inside, I sat down on the edge of the bed and just stared at myself in the mirror for a minute. Everything felt like it was coming down on me all at the same time. I had fallen for this man, and we'd had the most amazing sex ever, but there I was, still pregnant, still holding back from him, knowing that as soon as I told him, all of it would be over. I'd broken my word to myself, and as I sat there disappointed in myself, tears ran down my face.

I put my face in my hands and curled up in the center of the bed, unable to stop the flood of emotions. Blake made me feel so many things, so many complicated and crazy things, and I was powerless against him. One touch of his hand, one whisper, one kiss, and I melted right into him. All the strength and reserve that I prided myself on as a woman somehow was completely lost whenever I was with him. It was unbelievable, like I'd never experienced love before, and it was knocking me straight on my ass.

I didn't know what to do. I was pregnant with a child I knew he wasn't going to want. As soon as I told him, he wouldn't want me anymore either. I was completely and totally wrecked, and all it had taken was for him to make love to me one single time. This was going to be a disaster, a horrifying, life-altering disaster.

Chapter 31

Blake

I slammed my hand down on the desk and smiled big. The deal I had been working on for the last month had just come to fruition. Inez raced in with her hands clasped, waiting to hear the news. I gave her the thumbs-up, and she screamed in excitement. I raced forward, picked her up in the air, and hugged her tightly.

"This is so fantastic." I laughed. "I couldn't have done any of it without you. You set the whole thing up."

"And you knocked it out of the park," she said as I sat her back down on her feet. "We make a good team, even after all these years."

"We sure do," I said, walking back around my desk. "I knew I kept you on the payroll for a reason."

"Oh, and so you know, that bonus you gave me, that got me and Tom into our new house." she smiled. "I'm finally out of South Boston. We had been saving up for years."

"Well, congratulations," I said, laughing. "What an amazing freaking day. You know what? I think we should take the rest of the day off, with pay of course."

"I won't argue that. I'll get those contracts sent over first, though."

"Thank you so much," I said. "I'm going to bolt. I really want to go home."

"Of course, have a great evening," she said as I walked out of the office.

I was beyond excited. It was the first real deal I had made since my wife died. I felt like I was back on top again. When I got in the car, I grabbed my phone, hearing it buzz. It was Hollis letting me know he was in town and on his way over to the house. Having my best friend drop in for a surprise visit on a day like this only made things ten times better. I laughed to myself and shook my head, hoping that my streak of luck continued.

I stopped off at the store to grab some champagne and takeout from next door. There was no way I was going to make Aly cook tonight. I wanted her to celebrate with me. I wanted her to enjoy the night not as my nanny but as part of my life, a part that really made things come together. She was part of the reason I was able to bring myself to make this deal happen. If I had still been in the mindset I was in before she got here, I would have never even attempted the deal. I would have let it slip through my fingers like so many others.

When I got home, I parked in the driveway and jogged into the house, carrying all my goodies. I went into the kitchen and set it all on the counter, walking straight up to Aly and grabbing her face, planting a big kiss right on her. She laughed and swatted me with the towel.

"What was that for?"

"I made a really huge deal at work, and it's going to get the company back on the right track, plus some," I said with a smile.

"That's awesome, congratulations," she said excitedly, looking up as the doorbell rang. "Who is that?"

"Your brother, dropping in to surprise you." I smiled.

"Really?"

She rushed out of the kitchen and toward the front door with me trailing right behind her. I loved it when she got that excited. I just had to remember to keep my hands to myself while her brother was there. She flung open the door and launched into her brother's arms, hugging him tightly. She was so happy to see Hollis, and she stood there for a long time, just embracing him. I knew she missed her family and to see her happy like that really warmed my heart. At the same time, though, I wondered if she was having a hard time keeping the secret from him.

I knew when he was here last time it had affected her, and over time, that had gone away. Now that he was back, I worried the same guilt she felt before would start riding up inside of her. My intention was never to make her uncomfortable or unhappy. It was simply to keep everyone out of what we weren't even sure was something to tell them about. I wanted my son to be kept in the dark, too, and if it was made into a big deal, there was a good chance Cooper would catch wind of it. It would be difficult to tell her family but then tell them they couldn't meet my son.

We understood why it was important, but I really doubted anyone else would. Maybe Hollis, but that would only be if he didn't choke me out first. We'd just gotten over drama, and the last thing I wanted to do was bring more of it right back into the house and right back into our lives.

I pushed the thoughts to the side and greeted my best friend with a huge hug. He pulled back and laughed, surprised by such a happy greeting. We all walked into the living room where Cooper was, and he jumped up, running across the floor and into Hollis's arms. The kid really loved Hollis who had been one of the few steady people in his life since he was little.

"All right, I got champagne, takeout, and good news, so let's all sit down in the dining room and eat some food," I said, clapping my hands.

"I'll help get the food set out," Aly rushed off to the kitchen.

Cooper followed after her and grabbed the plates, napkins, and silverware while I grabbed the champagne glasses from the bar. We all sat down around the table and began to feast, laughing and talking loudly about our days. I wanted to tell them about the gig, even though I'd already told Aly, but I wanted them to settle down first.

"Uncle Hollis, are you staying long?"

"Longer than last time but only for a couple of hours," he said. "I have to get back to San Francisco. My company needs me."

"Maybe next time, you can stay a couple of days," Cooper said.

"Yes, that sounds like a fantastic idea," he replied. "I'll make sure I make that happen. So Blake, didn't you say you have an announcement?"

"I did" I laughed. "I signed a huge contract today with a client, maybe the biggest contract besides the one with the NFL."

"Is it a sports one?" Cooper asked.

"It is," I said excitedly. "And this one is with Major League Baseball."

"Wow," Aly said.

"That's awesome," Cooper yelled out.

"Good job, buddy," Hollis said, shaking his head. "Then a toast to Blake for getting back on his game and moving forward into a huge and bright future."

"Here, here," everyone said, including Cooper with his glass of milk.

I glanced over at Aly as she put her glass down, not actually taking a sip of the champagne. It was odd because I could have sworn I remembered her telling me she loved champagne. If not, I would have gotten her something else. I smiled at her and swallowed the drink in my mouth.

"What's wrong, Aly?" I said. "You don't like your champagne?"

"Are you kidding me?" Hollis laughed. "Champagne is like her favorite drink ever. You should have seen her when she was twenty-one at our cousin's wedding. I'm pretty sure she polished off a bottle all on her own. I really don't know how she does it considering it's like a freaking hangover in a bottle, though you do buy the good stuff."

I looked over at Aly and smiled sweetly, confused by the fact that she was looking down into her lap, her cheeks blushing red. I tried to change the subject, but Hollis had zeroed in on her, so all I could do was sit and wait for her to answer.

"I just don't want any today, thank you," she mumbled.

"Oh, come on," Hollis laughed. "You don't have to be afraid to drink in front of Blake just because he's your boss. This is a celebration and champagne's your favorite. Seriously, Blake, I've never seen her turn down a glass, no matter the kind."

I smiled and looked over at Aly watching her hand slip down over her belly. I squinted my eyes. Maybe she wasn't feeling well again. All it would have taken was one sip to get Hollis off her back, but she was adamantly refusing to even think about drinking that glass of champagne. Something wasn't sitting right with me, and I didn't know what it was. She had been acting strangely lately, though our sex had been better than ever, and she seemed insatiable. Something was up but I couldn't put my finger on it.

I excused Cooper from the table, telling him to go get himself ready for a bath and I'd be up to get the tub going in a minute.

"Hollis, please," she said with her teeth gritted.

"Come on, sis, don't be rude." He laughed. "Just a sip."

I could see the frustration building in her face. She was about to explode. I didn't want this evening to turn out badly, but I couldn't figure out why she was acting so strangely. Eventually, I put out my hand and chuckled.

"Hollis, it's all right. If she doesn't want the champagne, then she doesn't have to drink it," I said.

"No way, I want to know what's up with you," he said turning to her. "'Cuz something is definitely up."

"Look," she said, slamming her napkin down on her plate. "If you want it so badly, drink it yourself."

"Aly," Hollis said, taken back. "Why are you getting so upset?"

"I can't have it," she finally blurted out, standing up and marching from the room.

I stood up as she did but stayed there, watching her march off down the hallway and up the stairs. Suddenly, all the pieces fell into place and it felt like a punch in the gut. I carefully took my napkin from my lap and placed it on the table, in complete shock. I turned to go after her, but when I did, Hollis was standing right there, a look of rage and betrayal on his face.

"Hollis, I had no idea," I said, putting up my hands.

"You fucking bastard," he growled, rearing back and punching me square in the jaw. "I told you not to touch my fucking sister."

My vision hadn't even cleared from his first shot before Hollis was all over me.

Chapter 32

Aly

After yelling and marching from the room, I didn't even look back to see the look on Blake's face. I knew he would put it all together, and most likely, my brother would too, but at that point, I didn't give a damn. I'd had enough of all the secrets. It was already too much that I couldn't tell my family about Blake and me, but to keep the secret of the baby pushed me over the edge. It was something I'd been handling all on my own with no support and no one to talk to, and finally, I'd had enough. I lost it. I completely lost it.

I marched up the stairs, slowing down as I lost my breath. I didn't hear anyone follow after me, and that was good because I was tired of talking, tired of reasoning, and I knew with that revelation, I would have plenty of talking to do when I finally got home and faced the rest of my family. I walked into my room and sat down on the edge of the bed, wiping the tears away before I became a complete mess. Just then, I heard a commotion, shouting, and the sound of glass breaking. I stood up, pulling my eyebrows together and listening harder, trying to figure out what in the world was going on.

Suddenly, Cooper came running around the corner and straight into my room, a look of terror on his face. I bent down and looked at him, waiting for him to calm down enough to form a sentence. I wiped his hair out of his eyes and grabbed his shoulders.

"What's wrong?" I asked. "What's happened?"

"My dad and Uncle Hollis," he panted, "They're fighting."

"Oh, for God's sake," I said, shaking my head. "Okay, I'll go take care of this. I want you to go to your room and put on your headphones. Watch a movie on your laptop if you'd like."

"Is Dad okay?" he asked.

"Of course. Men sometimes get angry at each other, but you know your Uncle Hollis would never seriously hurt your dad. He loves him," I said. At least, I hoped I was right.

I walked Cooper to his room and watched as he put on headphones and started a movie. I smiled and closed the door, turning toward the loud banging downstairs. I rolled my eyes and marched back down the stairs and into the kitchen where Hollis was beating the shit out of Blake and Blake was giving as good as he was getting. I couldn't believe the two of them, acting like complete and total idiots.

"Stop it," I yelled at the top of my lungs getting their attention. "Both of you are acting like complete morons. I'm not some damsel in distress that needs the two of you fighting over my goddamn honor. Not to mention, you've scared the shit out of Cooper."

Both Hollis and Blake backed off each other, pulling themselves off the floor. I folded my arms over my chest and tapped my foot, pissed that I had to deal with this kind of asinine behavior. I looked over at Blake and surveyed the damage. He was already starting to get a black eye and blood was running down his chin from his lip. He had blood stains on the collar of his shirt. I turned and looked at Hollis who looked no better than Blake did at that moment.

"This is ridiculous," I said. "I'm a grown woman who made my own choices. I don't need my big brother coming in and beating up a guy for me."

I walked forward and stood there between the two of them, looking back and forth. On one side was the man I loved, who I couldn't be with, who just learned I was pregnant. On the other side was my older brother, the one sworn to protect my honor. If it hadn't been me in the middle, I might have thought the whole situation was sweet, but as it was, I did not.

I looked up at Hollis. "I'm the one who did something stupid. I'm the one who made a choice on a whim and now have to pay for that choice. I'm the one who's been holding this back out of fear. If you want to be angry with someone, either of you, be angry with me. Hollis, it's not only Blake's fault. We made a choice, an adult choice, and we made it together. Don't ruin your friendship over this."

"What friendship?" he scoffed.

"Oh stop it. You're just being an idiot. You two have been best friends since you were kids. So one mistake is going to ruin all of that? Don't be stupid Hollis." I could feel the emotions start to well up inside of me, and I wanted to get out of there before they overflowed. My crying would only make things worse, and now that it was all said and done, t couldn't be taken back.

"Blake," I said, turning toward him. "I'm sorry I kept this from you. It's not an excuse, but I was afraid to tell you. I know this isn't what we intended to happen. You just wanted to have a little bit of fun. I know you weren't looking for forever, and this was not my intention to trap you into something. I know you don't want to raise another baby."

Blake's jaw dropped open, and I could tell that his brain was so stunned by the news that he couldn't put two words together. It was better that way. I didn't need him making false promises just because my brother was there. I didn't need him telling me to stay because he felt obligated to. I was not an idiot. I knew how these kinds of things worked.

"Hollis," I said. "I want you to stop fighting with him. What is done is done, and we can't go back. At this point, I'd just like to get my things and have you take me home. I need to go and explain it all to Mom and Dad and start trying to figure out the rest of my life. I can't live in some fairy tale anymore. It's time for me to face reality.

Hollis glared over at Blake for a moment and then looked at me, softening his gaze. He didn't say a word, just nodded his head and wiped the blood from his chin. I sighed and turned, walking back to the stairs as quickly as I could. I didn't want either of them to say a word to me. I just wanted to get packed and get out of there. I had caused enough drama for one day and arguing or fighting more wasn't going to change anything.

I left the door to my room open as I grabbed my suitcase and started to pile my things into it. I ran my hand over the pregnancy test in the top pouch and sighed, saddened that this was how I was bringing a new life into the world. I shook my head and continued on, folding my things quickly and pulling out my second suitcase. I piled all my belongings inside and shut them both, zipping them up. I looked around the room quickly, trying to make sure I didn't leave anything behind. If I did, I was sure that Blake would put it in the mail for me.

I grabbed my purse and pulled out my wallet, making sure I had my driver's license, my cash, and my debit card. I shut my wallet and put it back in my purse, turning and walking over to my luggage. I reached up to turn off the light and stared at the room that just a little over two months before I had thought I was the luckiest girl in the world to stay in. Now, all I could do was run away from it, run back home with my tail between my legs and a lifelong souvenir of my trip with me.

I pulled one suitcase and picked up the lighter one, struggling down the stairs. I could see Hollis through the large windows at the front of the house, standing on the porch. Blake raced up the steps and took one of my bags, helping me down to the bottom. He looked desperate to speak, but I couldn't tell if he even knew what to say.

"Please, Aly," he begged. "Don't go, not now. Give me a chance to talk to you about this. Please."

"Stop," I said, shaking my head. "Right now, I just want to go home. I don't want you to make any promises to me because you think it's the right thing to do. I know you don't want more children Blake, you told me that flat out. If you want to have some sort of long distance relationship with this child then fine, but I won't let a baby grow up in a house where it isn't wanted."

"Aly, I didn't know…" he trailed off, dropping his hands to his side.

I picked up my suitcase and walked out the door, handing them to Hollis. I stood there for a moment, looking around the yard, remembering how beautiful I thought the place was when I first arrived. Hollis went and put the suitcases in the car while Blake stood right inside, his face in his hand, shaking his head back and forth. It really was a sad scene, not the one I intended to have, and part of me did feel bad for blurting it out like that, but I couldn't hold back any longer. Life had kicked me right in the gut.

"Will you wait a minute?" I asked Hollis. "I want to say goodbye to Cooper."

"Sure," he said.

"If that is all right with you," I said, turning to Blake.

He didn't say a word, just nodded his head, staring at the ground beneath us. I looked at him for a moment and then turned, going upstairs and opening Cooper's door. He was sitting there with his headphones off staring at me with tears in his eyes.

"You're leaving," he said, starting to cry.

"I'm so sorry," I said, bending down and hugging him tightly. "I don't want to leave you. It's not you at all. You are what kept me here this whole time. There are just some adult things that I can't explain and I need to deal with them back home. I just want you to remember that I love you, your dad loves no matter what mood he's in, and you're going to be okay."

"Thank you for coming here and making things better," he sniffled, his face in my shoulder.

"I'll see you again, I'm sure of it," I said, choking back tears.

I turned and raced from the room, unable to handle saying goodbye. Hollis was waiting outside and took my hand, walking me to his rental car. I looked back for only a moment and stared at Blake standing in the doorway, and for a moment, it looked like he was crying.

Chapter 33

Blake

I couldn't wrap my head around what happened. In the blink of an eye, my life had changed forever. I was told I was going to be a father again, and before I could even react, Aly was gone. The house was still, silent almost, and I could hear my heart barely beating in my chest. I spent all of Thursday holed up in the house, only leaving to take Cooper to and from school. I moped around, staring at the empty room that she was in the day before, wondering how everything had gotten so out of control so fast.

I'd started that day in such a good mood, landing a huge client, seeing my best friend for a surprise visit, and living on cloud nine. By the end of it, I was standing alone in the entryway to my house with a black eye, a busted lip, and crying child upstairs that I didn't know how to console. It wasn't fair for him. He had already lost so much, and he loved Aly. He had to say goodbye to another important woman in his life, and it was my fault because I'd been too stunned to fight. When he got home from school that Thursday, he didn't say anything at all, just went upstairs and shut his door.

I hadn't gone to work, calling out and telling Inez I was sick. I didn't have the heart to tell her I'd gone and dug myself a whole new hole to lay in. My house had become a mausoleum, a tribute to everything that was Aly. The kitchen was silent, the halls were silent, and even the birds didn't seem to come out that day. It was overcast outside, a gloomy day to fit my mood. I just stood in the living room staring out into the backyard, remembering all the times Aly stood right out there throwing the baseball back and forth with Cooper.

How could she have taken all the life in that house with her? We had been here before her, and we would be here after her, but when she left, everything fell into silence. I didn't get it. Why wouldn't she at least let me talk to her about the baby? I wasn't angry with her. It was a bit of a shock, yes, but not enough to warrant her picking up and leaving right then and there. Somewhere along the way, I'd given her the impression I didn't care about her, that I wasn't going to be there for her.

I spent twenty-four hours straight thinking about it, moping, sitting in that unbearable quiet. I replayed it over and over in my head, trying to figure out the exact moment I pushed her to that point. I beat myself up, I cried, I doubted everything about me as a person. But then I stopped like I could hear Aly's voice ringing out in my head. This was exactly what I had done when my wife died, only I took it and I rode it for an entire year. I did nothing with my time. I didn't shave, I barely ate, I didn't talk to my son, and I sank down lower and lower until there was barely anything left of me. It was Aly who'd brought me out. It was her who told me I couldn't do that to myself or to Cooper anymore.

That same advice had to be applied to this. I couldn't fall apart all over again, not with the kinds of steps I'd taken to make my life better and stronger. I felt like she was the glue that had held me together for all those weeks, but now I had to hold myself together. I had to take a step forward and decide to not let the anger and heartbreak overtake me. I had a little boy upstairs who was counting on that, praying I would be there for him through all of this. I couldn't let him down again. I had promised him that.

On Friday, when he got home from school, Cooper did the same thing, just walked up the stairs and closed his door. I went into the kitchen and pulled out the ice cream and made us both a bowl. Carefully, I carried them up the stairs and stood outside of his room, nervous to go inside. I had to do it, though. It was the most important part of all of it. If I couldn't be a strong father for one, how was I ever supposed to be strong for two? I knocked on the door and waited for Cooper to open it.

"Hey," he said, moping back into his room.

"Hey," I replied. "I brought you some ice cream."

"Thanks," he said, taking the bowl and setting it on his nightstand.

"Look, I know you're really upset because Aly left," I said. "And I know you don't understand it, but I need you to know it had nothing to do with you."

"Then what did it have to do with?" he said angrily. "Don't tell me I'm too young to understand."

"All right," I said. "Aly and I were seeing each other, and Uncle Hollis didn't know. We found out over dinner that she's going to have a baby."

"A baby?" Cooper asked, his eyes big and bright?

"Yes, my baby," I told him.

"Then why didn't you just marry her?" he asked like it made the most sense in the world. "Cooper." I chuckled. "It's not as simple as you think it is."

"Yes, it is," he said. "You adults just make it complicated. Do you love her?"

"Well …"

I sat there for a second staring at my son, thinking about his question. I shook my head and rubbed my face, laughing at the irony of how he got it and I didn't. My eight-year-old son was right. I did love her. I loved her very much. What an idiot I was.

"You are a wise little man," I said, shaking my head. "Damn, what have I done? I have really screwed things up this time."

"Yeah, but you can fix it," he said.

I took a deep breath and laid back on his bed, staring up at the ceiling. I did love Aly, and I had never actually told her. Hell, I had never even let her think she was anything other than a ready lay. I knew all along in the back of my mind that I had fallen for her. I'd known that when I finally said, fuck it, and started sleeping with her on a regular basis. When she was sick, I was scared for her. I wanted to take the pain from her. When she was sad, I wanted to make her happy in any way I knew how. When she was angry, I just wanted to kiss her and make it dissolve.

I could have told her that from the beginning. I could have expressed my feelings to her when I had the chance, and none of this would have turned out the way that it had. I made her feel like she was my play toy. How shitty of me was that? She had come into our home, embraced us even with our faults, pulled us together as a family, and I let her walk away from me. I let her run off with my child growing inside of her. She was part of our family, and so was that baby, and she belonged with us and us with her. I spent so much time trying to fight my feelings that I let her walk right out of my life.

"Dad," Cooper said, tugging me out of my thoughts. "Did you hear me? You have to fix this. She has my baby brother in her belly."

"How do you know it's a boy?"

"I don't. I'm just hoping." He smiled.

"Okay, hold on," I said, pulling out my phone.

I dialed Aly's number, but it only rang a couple of times and went straight to voice mail. I hung up and thought for a second before pulling up Hollis's number and pressing send. I knew the guy didn't want to talk to me, but I had to get in contact with Aly.

"What the fuck do you think you're doing calling my phone?" Hollis answered.

"I need you to calm down and hear me out," I said.

"Fuck you," he said, before hanging up the phone.

"That backfired, didn't it?" Cooper asked looking at me.

"Yeah," I said. "We need a plan. We need a plan that is seriously drastic. She's not going to want to talk to me easily, and her family will do everything they can to keep her from talking to me at this point. They think I'm a bad guy. They don't know I love her."

"But what are we supposed to do then?" Cooper sighed. "I mean, if you can't call her or video chat with her, how are you ever supposed to tell her how you feel? She isn't in Boston anymore."

I sat there thinking about it. It was obvious Aly wasn't going to pick up the phone any time soon. It was obvious her brother, my best friend, wasn't going to be the least bit helpful in getting me in touch with her. I couldn't wait to tell her how I felt. I'd waited too long already. I didn't want so much time to pass that she just gave up on us. She was the woman I wanted, and she had our child growing inside of her. We needed to fix this before it was too late. I wanted us to be a family, the four of us, and I knew Cooper wanted that too.

I stood up and started pacing the floor, running through ideas in my head. I could contact her on social media, but that was not only tacky but unreliable at best. It was as easy to ignore me on there as it was to ignore a phone call. I could call her parents, but I was pretty sure neither one of them was going to let me get within ten feet of her. They weren't going to understand. They were just going to see me as this older pervert who knocked up their daughter. No, none of those were going to work. I had to reach her, and it wasn't going to be possible from Boston. I stopped and looked over at Cooper.

"How would you like to see California?" I asked.

Chapter 34

Aly

I stood in the doorway, staring out at the street, the bridge far in the distance. My heart was aching, and my body felt like it was falling apart at the seams. I had told my parents when I got home, and instead of chastising me, they were actually very comforting. Even my hard-nosed father had hugged me tightly and told me everything would be okay.

"Come here, sweetie," my mom said, touching my shoulder.

I turned and leaned into her, resting my head on her like I did when I was a kid. I looked up at my sisters, all hovering in the doorway, looks of pity on their faces. My mom had her arms wrapped tightly around me, rocking me back and forth.

"Mom," I said. "I'm okay, I promise."

"You're right, dear," she said, not really listening. "Everything will be okay in the end. We'll have a beautiful little baby, you'll get your education, and you'll make it out there. Not every child grows up with a father, and most of them turn out just fine."

"I'm not keeping the baby from him," I groaned, feeling her squeezing even tighter. "Mom, I can't breathe."

Finally, she let go of me, and I gasped for air, putting my hand to my chest. My whole family was indignant about the situation, making plans for Blake's demise. I just shook my head, thankful for the support but hopeful they would lighten up a bit. Then my mother spoke.

"Screw that sonofabitch," she said. "He took advantage of a young, beautiful woman, played you, broke your heart, and knocked you up. He doesn't deserve to be anywhere near you or that child."

"Mom, please," I said, putting up my hands. "As much as I appreciate the solidarity, don't curse him like that. That man, whether you like it or not, is the father of your grandchild. Besides, he didn't take advantage of me. I went into the relationship with my eyes wide open. I wanted it as much as he did. We just weren't very smart about it from the beginning. We took a chance and threw caution to the wind, and this is what came out of it. I left on my own accord, and up to that moment, things were really amazing between us. We just didn't tell anyone because we didn't know where it was going to lead, and until we did, we didn't want Cooper to get his hopes up. He'd lost too much already, and we didn't need him to be hurt if things didn't work out. Though I have to say, we kind of screwed the pooch on that one because he got hurt anyway."

"I don't understand how you can be so calm about this," my mother said. "He let you and that baby walk right out those doors."

"I know in this situation you want to have someone to be angry with, and you don't want to be mad at me," I said. "But I'm not mad at anyone, not even Blake. He never made us out to be more than what it was. He never pledged himself to me, he never told me he loved me, and he never led me to believe we had a future. I know that kind of relationship is hard for you to understand because you have Dad, but it is what it is. Being mad at him is only going to make things harder during this entire process. I haven't decided how much I'm going to offer him to be a part of it, and I don't know how much he wants to be involved. But try to see this as a situation I got myself in as much as he did. This doesn't need to be a war."

"I will respect your feelings and try to keep my opinions to myself," she said, straightening my hair. "But just know that we're here for you, no matter what, even if he does turn into the man we all think he'll become."

"Thanks, Mom," I sighed, shaking my head.

I watched as my mom walked out of the room, summoning my sisters with her. Jackie stayed behind and walked in, shutting the door behind her. She rolled her eyes and chuckled at how our mother was behaving.

"I swear it's like she's ready to don her battle gear and walk into war," Jackie laughed. "I guess it's better than them guilt tripping you over it."

"Yeah, right now. Who knows what will happen ten minutes from now?" I said.

Jackie sat down next to me on the bed and let out a sigh. I pulled my hands up and buried my face in them, trying to get my head on straight. I couldn't believe everything had turned out like it had, but it had been my choice to get up and leave. I knew I would end up back at home eventually, sitting here listening to my family go nuts over everything, but I was hoping it would be a bit of a better situation than that. Jackie reached over and patted me on the back.

"Don't freak out," she said. "Everything's going to be just fine, and if not, you know you have like five people out there ready to go straight ninja on his ass."

I laughed and picked up my head, closing my eyes and leaning my head back. I let my body follow and lay back on the bed staring up at the ceiling. Blake's and Cooper's faces ran through my mind, and for a moment, I really missed them.

"I know it's going to be okay," I sighed. "Not once during this whole thing did I think my life was over. Well, maybe the first few minutes after I saw the test results and ran around looking for a hiding place for them. But other than that, I knew I would be okay. I can finish college online while I take care of the baby. If I can be a nanny and still get through school, I can be a mom and do it too. As far as financial stuff, I'm not the least bit concerned. I'm positive Blake will make sure I'm financially sound. Just because he doesn't want to raise another child doesn't mean he won't support one."

"Well," she said, slapping my leg and standing up. "At least he doesn't sound like a complete tool bag. I'm gonna go grab a snack, you want to come?"

"No, I'm just going to lay here for a bit and rest," I said. "I'm tired of everyone staring at me like I'm infected with a deadly virus."

"I mean, that *is* my view on children, but to each their own." Jackie laughed. "I'll be out here if you need me."

"Thanks." I smiled.

When Jackie left, I continued to lay there, still staring up at the old glow in the dark stars I had put on my ceiling when I was no more than eight years old. Just the same age as Cooper. It was the same room I had grown up in, lay thinking about my first kiss in, gushed to my sister about my first love in, and cried over my first heartbreak in. I had grown up right there, and I knew it was time I moved on. I loved my parents, I really did, but I could already tell they were going to drive me absolutely nuts. Why did I have to be the first kid to pop out a grandchild? I was going to be like birth control for the others after seeing how psychotic my mother got over the baby. I guess I shouldn't complain, though. I had a really strong support system with more love for my child than it would ever need or want.

Still, I needed to find my own place before the baby came. There was no way I was going to survive living there with my child and my mother. She would suffocate the hell out of both of us. I could see it now, my mother pointing out every wrong thing I did from how to hold to how to nurse. She would become the mother hen I wanted to choke out, and our relationship would ultimately be hurt by it. No, it was time I stepped out on my own and raised my little family, even if it was just the two of us. Then, at least, I could start moving forward.

My sisters could come visit, my brother could come torture me, and if Blake wanted to see the baby, he would have a safe place to come and not be attacked by my parents and siblings. It was a no-brainer. I would start looking for a place as soon as I could, or at least as soon as I figured things out with Blake.

I sat up on the bed and shook the dizziness from my head. I had only been there for a day, and I was already bored out of my mind. I walked over and picked up my phone, turning it on for the first time since I had left. I knew Blake would try to call, but I was not in the right kind of mindset to deal with it when I had to deal with my entire family first, especially when my mom called a family emergency over it.

When my phone had loaded, the voice mail beeped, showing me I had two missed messages. I didn't know how many times he called, but I was surprised that there were only two messages in the box. I pressed send and put in the code, putting the phone to my ear and grimacing. I wasn't sure what I was going to hear.

"Aly, please call me back. We really need to talk," Blake said, sounding sad

I took a deep breath and waited for the next one to load. It made me wonder how he was doing over there in Boston, how he was faring with me leaving like I did, or if it even affected him at all.

"Aly, it's Blake. I've tried to call you several times, and I understand you're taking a step back, but I'm not going to let you walk away like this. It's too important."

Chapter 35

Blake

I smiled at Cooper as he gawked out the window of the plane, mesmerized by the clouds passing by the window so quickly. We were on our descent into San Francisco Airport after a very long flight from Boston. It was the first time Cooper was flying out there since our lives had been so busy back home. He had obviously gotten to know my parents, but it had been from them coming to see us in Boston. I would be pretty excited to show Cooper around if it weren't for the circumstances.

When we got off the plane, I rented a car, and we headed off to my parents' house in the hills. They lived right beyond the city limits of San Francisco now, having moved from when I was a kid. Cooper was excited to see them and even more excited when he got off the plane and the sun was shining. It was still pretty chilly out here but nowhere as near as bad as Boston was. When we pulled up at my parents' place, I took a deep breath, knowing I was going to have to explain everything to them. They weren't necessarily judgmental people, but they had their thoughts on the way things were supposed to be, and in their old age, they weren't wavering on them.

I pulled up out front and parked the car, watching Cooper hop out, run across the driveway, and jump into his grandmother's arms. I slowly got out and stretched, walking over and shaking my father's hand. My mom walked up and wrapped her arms around me, squeezing me tightly.

"It's really good to see you, son," she said. "You look so good, like you've been eating again."

"I have." I chuckled.

"I do have to say I'm very disappointed it took this long for you to bring Cooper out here to San Francisco," she said.

"Leave him alone, Joyce," my father said. "He's a bigshot out there. He owns a huge company, and he has some serious responsibilities. I don't mind Boston, anyway. They have good chowder."

My mother shook her head as we walked arm in arm into the house. It was big, a lot bigger than the one I grew up in, and I was glad to see my parents were doing well. We walked into the living room and I set down the luggage, smiling over at my mother.

"I'm sorry we don't get out here more often. Things have been up and down the last couple of years." I smiled. "But I do appreciate you putting me and Cooper up on such short notice."

"Don't be silly," my mom said, hugging me again and then Cooper. "You're my boys. You're welcome here anytime. You can just show up even. You don't even need to call."

"Come on," my dad said, picking up the luggage. "Your room is in the basement. I had it converted into a guest room and study area. I do all my great thinking down here."

Cooper giggled, and my mom rolled her eyes, throwing her hands up in the air. Besides the fact they had aged quite a bit since the last time I saw them, nothing really had changed. I had to admit it was nice to be around family again, something I'd pushed away when my wife died. They understood, but that didn't make it right. I should have been there and let them be there for me. Either way, I was here now, and I had some seriously important business to attend to.

Cooper and I got settled into our place for the evening and then went upstairs to have dinner with my parents. My mom overcooked as usual, but Cooper was in the seventh heaven with a giant plate full of homemade macaroni and cheese. As we sat and ate, I knew the question was coming, and I was trying to formulate what my response would be ahead of time.

"So, why are you coming to San Francisco on such short notice?" my mom asked, right on cue. I had no choice really but to get it all out and quickly before I lost my nerve.

"Well, it's a tricky situation," I said, wiping my mouth. "I hired Hollis's little sister, Aly, to be Cooper's nanny."

"Aly," my mom repeated. "Oh, yes, the baby. How old is she now?"

"Twenty-three," I replied. "Anyway, while she was there, things happened, and I fell in love with her. Last week, during dinner with Hollis, we found out she was pregnant."

"What?" my mother said, dropping her fork.

"Yeah, but I screwed it up, and in the end, she ran off back here to San Francisco," I said. "I never told her how I felt about her, and I guess it seemed to her like I really didn't care about her, which isn't at all true. She was the best thing that's happened to us in a long time. So, I'm here to fix things, to make things right, and to make us a family like we should be. I'm going to be a dad again and Cooper a big brother, and I can't let her just run off."

"Well, this is more than a surprise," my mother said, leaning back. "But I'm proud of you for stepping up and admitting when you're wrong. Now, I'm not too happy you're messing around with such a young woman, but I'm old-school in that way. Nonetheless, with a baby on the way, and if you truly love her, I stand behind you. God knows, after everything you've been through, both of you, you deserve a little sunshine in your life. How exactly do you plan on getting her back?"

"That I haven't exactly worked all the way out," I chuckled. "We just knew that for me to do it, I had to come here and see her face-to-face. She wouldn't answer my calls, and her brother won't let me talk to her, so I didn't want this to go unchecked for too long. I need her to know I love her, and I need to make things right between us, not just for the baby but because I want her in our lives."

"How do you feel, Cooper?" my mom asked.

"I love her. She's awesome," he smiled. "And her and my dad, make a really good team. She brought him back from the dead."

Everyone laughed at Cooper's explanation of how I was, but in reality, he was pretty spot on. I was barely breathing at that point, just trying to make it through the day so I could go back home and sulk there instead of in my office. It made me a little sad that my son saw all of that, but thankful that I wasn't in that place anymore.

"He's right," I said. "Aly breathed life into our home, into mine and Cooper's relationship, and into my own self."

"You know," my dad said, winking at my mom. "Jewelry always works when you've messed up bad. Trust me. I speak from experience."

"He sure does. I had to buy a third jewelry box last year." She laughed. "But I love him to the ends of the earth anyway."

"Noted," I said, shaking my head. "It was actually going to be my first stop in the morning when I head over to see her."

We sat and finished dinner, talking about the weather, about the family, and all the other things we tried to catch up on when it had been a long time between visits. Cooper told them all about school, his robotics team, and the lock-in he went to a couple of weeks back. It was a really good visit with them, and I was thankful I had them around. Around eight, my parents retired to their bedroom to watch "their shows" and go to bed. Cooper and I went downstairs and unpacked before lounging on the bed and flipping on the television.

"Dad?" Cooper asked.

"Yeah, bud," I said, muting the TV.

"So, if you go tomorrow and Aly forgives you, and she feels loves you too, then what will happen next?" he asked.

"Well, that's hard to say," I said. "She might come back to Boston with us, she might want us to come to California, or we might figure out a back and forth until we get settled. Ideally, I would want her to stay with us, no matter what the location is."

"Will you two get married?" he asked.

"I was thinking about it." I smiled. "That was one of the pieces of jewelry I was thinking about buying tomorrow. Why? How would you feel about that?"

He was quiet for a moment before answering. "I really love Aly like a mom. I would be okay with her being my there every day with us. I know she's not my real mom but I think my real mom would be happy that Aly loves us."

"That's a very mature way to look at that, son," I said, hugging him tightly. "And I know you're right. Wherever your mom is, she knows how much you love her, and she'll be happy to know someone is taking care of you as good as she would."

"Do you ever miss Mom?" he asked.

"Sometimes," I said.

"Me too. Okay," he said, snuggling down in the bed next to me. "Good night."

"Night, buddy," I replied, flipping off the light.

I turned over on my side and laid my head on the pillow, staring into the darkness of the room. I knew it was going to be hard for me to get any kind of sleep, but I had to at least try. I was already nervous about the next day, and I hadn't even settled in yet. It was going to be a difficult conversation, especially with her whole family betting against me, but if I knew Aly like I thought I did, she would make up her own mind when it came to our life together.

After everything, it took her leaving for me to realize she was the woman for me. She was the woman I wanted to grow old with, to help me raise my son, and to raise *our* baby with. I was determined to get her back, no matter what.

Chapter 36

Aly

I had only been home a few days, and I was about to tear out my eyeballs. I just wanted some peace and quiet, just someone to shut up. When I lived in this house before, my sisters and brother never came around, but now it was like they were camping out. Just that morning, I'd gone out to the kitchen super early to get a cup of coffee, and there they were eating breakfast and talking up a storm. I loved my family, I really did, but it was hard to focus when they were constantly talking about me, my personal life, or Blake in some way. I knew not much happened in our family, so my situation was like Jerry Springer, but seriously, it was getting old.

I had started locking myself in my room, just to not hear them. They all thought I was depressed, but little did they know, they were the ones causing an issue. I tried to get out of the house for a little while, telling my mom I had to get some things from the store, but that failed since she jumped in the passenger seat and talked the entire time we were gone. I had this feeling they all decided I shouldn't be left alone, which was why every two hours on the dot someone different came knocking on my bedroom door to check on me. I felt like I was living in the crazy house only the doctors were the crazy ones.

Hunger was beating me up, though, and I knew my mom had just finished dinner. I sighed and pulled on my sweatshirt jacket, zipping it up to my chin and pulling the hood. I walked out of my room and was instantly greeted by my brother, who seemed to be just standing there.

"It's quiet in here," I said, reveling in the near silence for a moment.

"Yeah, the girls went bowling tonight." He laughed. "They were going to invite you, but mom told them you were too fragile."

"Too fragile to throw a five-pound ball down a hall and hit stuff?" I scoffed. "This isn't 1937 for Christ sake Hollis."

"It's okay," he said, putting his arm around me and walking me to the kitchen. "You can hang out with me."

"Joy," I said sarcastically.

"Hey, look who's up," my dad said as I walked around the corner. "Hi, sweetie."

"Hi, Daddy," I said, kissing him on the cheek and sitting down at the table.

"I made spaghetti tonight," my mom said, setting the bowl of noodles on the table. "I hope that agrees with your tummy."

"I think I'll prevail," I said with a sarcastic smile.

"So, I was thinking, doll," my dad said. "How about I go find Blake and punch him square in the nose?"

"Too late, dad," Hollis boasted. "I already beat you to him."

I sat there with my eyes squinted just watching the two of them laugh it up. It was like Blake went from the man of the year to the worst person in the world because he did what a million other men did. It was really, really getting old.

"I know," my dad laughed. "We could go stuff potatoes in the tailpipe of his pretty cars."

"And shaving cream the hood," my brother laughed. "But I don't know. The dude's loaded. He would just throw it away and get a new one."

"I sure do hate people like that," my mother chimed in. "They don't appreciate anything, and I know his mother didn't teach him to be like that."

I leaned my elbow on the table and rubbed my head, rolling my eyes into the back of it. I sat there for another thirty minutes, eating my spaghetti and listening to my parents and brother make a list of all the things they would do to Blake. All the things I knew they would never actually do, but that didn't stop them from talking about it. It was driving me batshit crazy. Finally, I got so fed up, I slammed my fork down on my plate and stood up, throwing my hands into the air.

"You are all freaking crazy," I yelled, turning and stomping away.

"Sheesh, what's wrong with her?" I heard my brother say.

"Hormones, dear," my mom whispered.

I growled, opening my bedroom door and slamming it behind me. I shook my head, pacing the floor back and forth. I needed space, air, anything that would make me feel like the room wasn't closing in around me. I turned quickly and looked back at my window, tapping my foot for a moment. I changed my clothes and put on some shoes before opening my window, slipping out, and shimmying down the trellis. I jumped the last two feet and landed, looking around like James Bond. I used to sneak out the window all the time when I was a kid, and my parents had never caught me. They always just thought I was the good child, but I was more like the smart child, never getting caught. It was, however, pretty sad that I had to, at twenty-three-years-old and about to be a mother, sneak out of my bedroom through the window.

I crept passed the window, poking my head up to watch my parents eating chocolate cake while my brother found Wheel of Fortune for them on the television. I reached in my pocket and pulled out my debit card and some cash, glad I'd chosen those pants because getting back up to the window was a very interesting prospect, something I didn't really think through before I jumped out.

I shrugged, figuring I would deal with it later and headed out toward town. Luckily, my parents lived in a flatter area of San Francisco, so I didn't have to brave too many crazy inclines. I walked around town, window shopping, and just enjoying the evening air and the freedom. I stopped at my favorite food truck and got a freshly squeezed juice before continuing on. As I walked, I thought about what had happened, and I began to wonder if I'd made the right choice. What if I had done a stupid thing? At first, I shook my head, telling myself I made the best decision for me, and that I was just having buyer's remorse because my family was so insane.

However, the farther I walked, the happier couples I saw walking along, and the more I cleared my head, I started to change my mind about it. I loved Blake, and though I made the assumption that he didn't love me, I never even stopped to find that out. I was having his child, so I knew I would see him again, but what if I'd made the wrong choice and couldn't go back and change it? What if he moved on, and I was left behind?

I had dropped an atom bomb on his ass in the middle of dinner with my brother. I had shocked the hell out of him, and before he could even chase after me, my brother was punching him right in the face. He'd had absolutely no time to process what I said, no time to think about it, and no time to respond. I literally told him, got up, and ran away like a scared little child. I backed him into a corner, and then I split, and he was left shocked, confused, and unable to even get a hold of me by phone. Not to mention he had to tend to his son, who I'd also walked out on.

"Oh God," I groaned, stopping on the sidewalk and looking out at the bridge. I hadn't only walked out on Blake, but I'd walked out on Cooper, too, and the kid didn't even know what was going on. If that wasn't fucked up, I didn't know what was. I'd made a rash decision, I panicked, and in that panic, I left a wake of heartache, including an eight-year-old little boy. I shook my head and tossed my juice cup in the trash can, feeling like a total asshole and a coward to boot. I couldn't bear hearing Blake tell me he didn't love me, so instead, I'd bolted.

I walked along the sidewalk until I came to the overlook, one of my favorite views of the bay and the bridge. It was starting to get dark out, and the lights on the bridge shimmered and shined in the distance. I really did love California. It was so beautiful and always had a way of calming me in my deepest storms. I reached into my pocket and pulled out my phone, leaning forward on the railing and looking down through my texts. Blake had texted me several times asking me to call, but I hadn't responded. Today was the first day I hadn't gotten a call or a text from him. I figured if I was coming to this epiphany, then it meant something, and I needed to talk to him.

I nodded and scrolled through my phone, stopping on his number. My finger hovered over the call button as I fought myself on whether to call him or not. Finally, I pressed send and pulled the phone up to my ear. It rang and rang, but nobody answered. I hung up before it went to voice mail and opened a new text.

"I'm sorry. Can we talk?" I texted him.

I sent the message and looked out at the bridge, hoping beyond hope that he would at least text me back. I stood there for over an hour, but he never texted me back, and it made my heart sink into my stomach. I turned and started back toward home, figuring my parents were probably in bed by then. Either way, I needed to get home and get some rest.

I thought about Blake the entire way back, and by the time I had reached the house, I had come to one very important conclusion. What I needed to do was really simple. I needed to go back to Boston and face Blake. He deserved the chance to talk to me, and he deserved the right to help make the best decision for him about the baby. I wanted him to be part of our child's life, regardless of whether he wanted to be in mine or not. When he wasn't depressed, he was a really good father, and I didn't want to raise a child who didn't know their father. In the perfect world, we would be a family, me, Blake, Cooper, and the baby, but at this point, I wasn't sure if it was even in the cards.

I got back to the house and sighed in relief, finding the front door key under the pot like it had been my whole life. I opened the door and tiptoed through the darkness, going into my room and shutting the door carefully. Everyone was in bed, which was perfect because I was ready to jump a plane back to Boston.

Chapter 37

Blake

When I woke up that morning, I had butterflies in my stomach. I rolled over in the bed, but Cooper was already upstairs, and I could hear him talking to my mom. I got out of bed and jumped in the shower before getting ready to see Aly. I picked out my clothes carefully, brushed my hair, my teeth, and shaved my face. When I was done with that, I spritzed some cologne on and went upstairs.

"I'm heading out," I said.

"Oh, honey, good luck." She smiled. "We'll be here when you get back."

"Good luck, Dad," Cooper said, motioning for me to bend down and then grabbing my cheeks. "Tell her you love her, you can't live without her, and then kiss her right on the lips. That gets them every time."

"I'm not sure how you know that, but okay." I laughed.

I waved goodbye as I headed over to the jewelry store. I spent about an hour looking through every ring they had until I found the perfect one. It was a fluke, really. I thought I'd decided on one, and as I was walking to the register, I saw this giant square diamond in the middle of the watches. I called the woman over, and she said it must have dropped in there during a fitting. It was the perfect ring, and I could already see it proudly displayed on Aly's hand. They put it in a box and stuck it in my sports coat pocket, signing my credit card receipt and heading back out to the car.

I thought about grabbing a coffee, but with my luck, I'd end up spilling it on myself. I was awake enough as it was, so I put the car in drive and headed over to Aly's parents' house. I pulled up to the house and looked over, my nerves growing until I could feel them in my throat. I turned off my dad's truck and sat there, trying to figure out exactly what I was going to say to her. I wanted it to be perfect, I didn't want to fumble through it, and I wanted Aly to know how much I loved her. I practiced what I was going to say over and over again, talking to the steering wheel. A woman pushing a stroller slowly walked by staring at me. I waved and awkwardly smiled, and she shook her head and walked away quickly.

Great, if it wasn't bad enough, now her neighbors were going to think I was some whack job sitting in the truck talking to myself. I had about gotten my speech down when I heard a car pulling up behind me. I looked up in the rearview mirror and saw Hollis putting his car in park and throwing his door open. He looked pissed, and I knew I was going to struggle through that conversation. I just hoped he didn't punch me again. He stalked forward toward the truck, and I sighed, taking the keys out of the ignition and opening the door. I climbed out and turned toward him, putting my hands up in the air in surrender.

"Of all the people to show up here, you have to be out of your mind," Hollis growled. "I thought I told you to fuck off!"

"You did," I said, holding up my hands. "You did, and I heard you, but I'm afraid it's not that easy. Your sister is pregnant with my child."

"I'm going to enjoy knocking the fucking shit out of you," Hollis growled, stepping toward me with his fist raised.

"Wait, wait, wait," I said, putting my hands up higher. "Before you hit me, you have to know something really important, something I left out last time that I saw you."

"What?" he yelled.

"I love her," I shouted. "I love her more than I've ever loved any other woman in my life. I have to admit I may have been a little slow on the uptake, but she's the only woman in the world for me. I want to marry her, I want to make her my wife and I want to raise our child and Cooper together. I've been through a lot in the last year, and when Aly came into my life, she was like a ray of sunshine I'd never experienced before. She made the world brighter for me, for Cooper, and for everything she touched around us. When she left me, she took the life from our home, and it made me realize it wasn't me getting better that made our home a wonderful place, it was that Aly was there. I fell in love with her long before I knew I had. I don't want to go through this life without her, Hollis. I want her to grow old with me, to teach Cooper how to be a good man, to teach me how to be a better man. I didn't come here to make empty promises. I came here to win back the love of my life."

Hollis paused just long enough for me to think that he'd changed his mind. Slowly, I lowered my hands and stood up straight, wanting desperately for him to know how much I loved her. Without him, I would have never even reunited with her in the first place. He was an important part to our story, and he was still my best friend, no matter how angry he was at me. I stared at him for a moment and then flinched as his fist hit me right across the chin, knocking me backward onto my ass.

I groaned, rubbing my face and shaking my head, trying to straighten out my vision. He had one hell of a right cross, that was for damn sure. I was a big guy, but he could have seriously knocked me out had he put his weight behind it. When my vision settled, I looked up at him, moving my jaw from side to side.

"You still deserved that," he said, pointing down at me, his voice softening.

"You're probably right," I said, nodding my head. "But can you please let me try to win her back now?"

"I'm not the only one standing in your way," he said. "And my father is not as nearly as nice as I am."

"I remember," I sighed.

Hollis rolled his eyes and reached his hand down. I looked at it for a second and then took it, letting him help me to my feet. He looked me up and down, still not trusting me, but at least he wasn't punching me over and over in the face like last time. I guess it all had to start somewhere, and as long as it got me in the house, I was fine with it.

"All right," he said. "But you can't just walk in there and expect my parents to step out of the way."

"I understand," I said.

Hollis nodded and started toward the front door with me trailing quietly behind him. I fiddled with my jacket, smoothed down my shirt, and brushed the gravel off my pants. I was sweating bullets, nervous as hell to face her family. I had to do it, though. It was important that I had their approval, just as important as it was to get Aly's. Hollis's family knew me. They watched me grow up from a boy to a teenager to a man. They were at my wedding, and they were at my wife's funeral. They had trusted me, and I had broken that trust in the worst way. For me to have any chance of fixing things with Aly, I first had to fix things with her family.

They were a stubborn bunch of people, and it would be a fight to get them back on my side. They were a tight-knit family, and when someone messed with one of them, they messed with all of them. On top of that, I had managed to pick the baby of the family to hurt, which made things ten times worse. Hollis stopped at the front door and turned around, looking me in the face.

"And you are one hundred percent sure you want to go into the snake pit?" he asked.

"Yes," I said, nodding my head. "It's the only way I even have a chance at getting Aly back, and I'll do anything to make that happen."

"Alright." He shrugged. "It's your funeral, but don't say I didn't warn you first."

I nodded my head as he opened the front door and stepped inside. He turned and put his hand up, motioning for me to stay there right inside the door. I nodded again, wiping my forehead and turned, closing the door behind me. I stood and watched as Hollis disappeared into the kitchen. I could hear him talking to someone, or multiple someones, but I couldn't tell exactly who it was. I looked around, noticing pictures of Aly when she was little, something I had never noticed in the million times I'd been inside their house.

Finally, after about five minutes, Hollis's father came walking around the corner, wiping his mouth with a napkin. He breathed deeply, skulking across the living room, and for a minute, I thought he was going to hit me too. He stopped midway to me and stared as his wife came scrambling up beside him, giving me a look of death. I nodded my head and opened my mouth to talk, but Hollis shook his head in the background. I closed my mouth and nodded at them instead.

"Aly isn't here," he said firmly.

"I think it's important I talk to you first anyway," I said. "I spent the last few days going over and over in my head what I would say to Aly if I had the chance. I came up with speech after speech, some heartwarming, some assertive, and some were, honestly, just really pathetic. I gave one of the better ones to your son out there on the street. That being said, to put it all down in simple terms, I love Aly. I love her with everything in me. I know it took me too long to figure that out, but that doesn't change the fact that she's the only woman in the world that I want to be with."

"You should have thought about that before she left," Hollis chimed in.

"You're right, I should have," I said. "But I didn't so I'm here now, standing here begging for another chance. I know I'm much older than Aly, and probably too old in your eyes. And I know I live way too far away as well because you're all so close. And I know that I already have a son, but not one of those things changes the fact that at the end of the day, Aly is the only woman I want standing beside me, helping me raise my children, loving me as I'm loving her. Love is strange, and it doesn't always make sense or come at the right time, but I cannot walk away from here without knowing one hundred percent that Aly doesn't love me and that she doesn't want to be with me. I have to try, and I am asking that you let me."

That was it, and now I had to face the firing squad.

Chapter 38

Aly

Before the sun was even fully over the horizon, I had snuck back out to take an early morning walk. I loved San Francisco in the morning when the trolleys were running full-speed, the fog was burning off, and the street vendors sold croissants. I used to go out three or four times a week to clear my head, just walk the pathways, watching the people hustling and bustling through the town. It had become my ritual and the only thing I was really enjoying after coming back. Blake was still strongly on my mind, and I woke up thinking about him. I tried to call him again when I went out, but it only rang twice before going straight to message.

It was nearing eleven in the morning when I made my way back to the house. As I approached, I slowed down, noticing an unfamiliar truck parked in front of my brother's car on the street. It had California plates, but I'd never seen the truck before. I took a bite of my croissant and shrugged my shoulders. Apparently, my house had turned into the one stop shop for everyone in town while I was gone. Maybe they were my mom's friends coming to wish me luck in my quest through single motherhood. I sighed and walked up to the front door, pausing as I heard voices right inside. The voice was familiar, but I was sure I was mistaken.

I carefully turned the doorknob and crept in, looking up to see Blake standing with his back to me, telling my parents exactly how he felt about me. He hadn't heard me come in, too focused on what he was saying, but every word was music to my ears. He loved me. He actually said it out loud, and I thought it would only be in my dreams. When he finished, I nodded at my father, reaching up and touching Blake on the shoulder. He turned around and stared at me wide-eyed and all I could do was smile. We stood there for several moments, just looking at each other, both of us not believing that we were actually in front of each other again.

"I love you too," I finally said.

"Ha," He laughed. "Ha ha!"

I giggled and screeched as he lunged forward and wrapped me up in his arms, staring at me for a moment before pressing his lips against mine, right in front of the whole family. I smiled as he kissed me, wrapping my arms around his neck and kissing him back. It felt so good to be in his embrace, to feel him close to me again. I loved him so much, and I was so relieved that he came for me. We continued to kiss until I heard my father in the background faking a cough.

"Sorry, sir," he said, pulling away but keeping his arm around my waist.

"She loves him," Hollis whispered in my dad's ear.

"Yes, yes," my father said, stepping forward and adjusting his pants. "It's all well and good that they love each other, but there's still a lot for them to talk about. There is more than just you two to worry about here. There's Blake's son and the new baby as well. I understand it all starts with love, but I think it's important for the two of you to hash out everything else as well. There are a lot of decisions to be made, and there's not a lot of room for error with it. I guess I can say we appreciate you coming to us first."

He turned around and looked at my family, blinking his eyes at them, assuming they caught his drift. My mother stared at him blankly and so did my brother. I giggled to myself as my father sighed, motioning with his hands for them to clear out of the room. He turned back and nodded over at me giving me a wink. I knew then that everything was going to be okay, that all my father wanted was for me to be happy and taken care of. Blake had stood in front of them, quivering in his shoes, spilling his heart out in hope of just the chance to talk to me. It was literally the most romantic thing I had ever seen, and it was directed at me. When we were finally alone again, he turned back around and kissed me one more time, acting like a kid. I laughed, feeling the excitement in the air, knowing that we both felt the same way toward each other.

I took his hand and led him over to the couch in the middle of the room. We both sat down close to one another. He reached over and pulled me into his lap, wrapping his arms around my waist and pressing his forehead against mine. For several moments, we just sat there like that, enjoying being that close to one another again. I had missed him so much, and this was the first time we'd been alone since I was at his house. I didn't know whether to hug him, kiss him, or cry. My emotions were wildly out of whack, and I knew it was the hormones, but it made it difficult to really think straight.

"I tried to call you," I said.

"You did?" he asked. "Oh, I turned my phone off on the plane and guess I forgot to turn it back on when we landed. It's still in my carry-on back at my parents' house."

"I thought you just didn't want to talk to me," I said with a smile.

"All I wanted to do was talk to you," he said. "I couldn't get you off my mind."

"You either," I replied.

"I have to tell you so that another minute doesn't go by without me making it right," he said. "I'm sorry for the way I treated you, or better than that, for the way I didn't treat you. Never once in my mind did I think of you as just a woman to sleep with, as a toy, or as a convenience. I fell for you almost instantly, but I fought myself on it and didn't fully recognize the fact until you were gone and my son pointed it out to me. I'd been hiding those feelings, pushing them to the side because I was scared. I should have treated you with more respect, shown you how much I cared about you, told you I sat at work every day thinking about you. I should have said you gave me butterflies the first time I saw you in the airport and that I couldn't stop thinking about that little red tank top and frying pan."

"Oh God." I giggled. "That was mortifying."

"That was the best night of my life." He laughed. "It was exactly what needed to happen to push me from my shell, to open me up to something other than grief. You saved me from all of that, and for that alone, I owe you an eternity of love."

"That's one hell of a speech," I said, drying the tear from my eye. "And while we're at it, I have something to say too."

"All right," he said, sitting up straight. "I'm all ears."

"I'm sorry for not telling you about the baby," I said, watching him shake his head. "Really, I knew about it for days before I let it out, and I should have come to you straight away."

"No, don't apologize for that," he said. "I was careless with my words. I didn't think things through when I should have. You came to me and asked me about kids, about families, and marriage, and I answered it without even thinking. I answered it based on knee-jerk emotion, not real thought. To be honest with you, I don't care if we have ten kids as long as you're by my side. We can build a football team if you want."

"Whoa," I laughed. "Slow down. How about I get through this first pregnancy, the poopy diapers, the late nights, and then we can discuss more kids."

He laughed. "I mean it, I would have as many as you wanted, as long as the two of us were there together as a family."

"You mean the three of us."

"No, wait. I mean the four of us," he said, laughing. "I've done given our kids away and scooped you off to a deserted island."

"Speaking of Cooper, did you talk to him about all of this?"

"More like *he* gave *me* a talking to." He laughed. "He knew I loved you before I even knew I loved you. And he's happy about this. He told me he loves you, and he'd be okay with having you in our lives because he knows wherever his mom is, she would be glad someone was taking care of him as good as she was."

"Aw," I said, another tear rolling down my cheek. "That makes everything so much more perfect. I was terrified he wouldn't want me in his life like that. I was worried he would think I was trying to take her place. I fell in love with Cooper before I even fell for you. He is the sweetest, kindest little boy I have ever met. We get along so well, and I've missed him so much. I was terrified I'd damaged him by leaving like that. I felt like such an asshole."

"Yeah, well, rest assured, he was not letting it go down like that," he said. "He helped me orchestrate this whole thing, coming to get you back. He's at my parents' house right now."

"He came with you?" I smiled. "What about school?"

"Meh," he scoffed. "He's a straight-A student who never misses school. He'll be fine. He deserved a vacation anyway, and he needed to see my parents. They're getting older, and I never brought Cooper to California."

"Well, I'm glad you did, and I can't wait to see him and give him a big hug and a thank-you for setting his dad straight." I giggled.

"I know, right?" he said, taking a deep breath and looking around.

I stared straight at him watching the laugh lines on his face as he glanced around the room. I loved this man so much, and I knew I wanted to spend the rest of my life with him. This had to be the best surprise ever, and now all I wanted to do was get him alone.

"Hey," I said, pulling his chin toward mine. "Do you wanna get out of here? Maybe go somewhere where we can be alone?"

"You read my mind." He chuckled. "Should I say goodbye to your folks?"

"Nah," I whispered, getting up and grabbing his hand.

We tiptoed through the house and out the front door, holding hands as we ran through the yard toward his truck. We jumped inside and laughed, feeling like we'd broken free from jail. I put my hand up and twirled it through the hair on the nape of his neck as he put the truck in drive and headed out.

Chapter 39

Blake

I drove through the city, one arm around Aly, the other on the steering wheel. She scooted closer to me and laid her head on my shoulder, the smell of her vanilla and lavender body spray wafting into the air. It was like being home again, wrapped in each other's arms, dying to be alone together. Only now, there were no secrets, no questions, everything was out in the open, and I knew I loved her, and I knew she loved me just as much. It had been the picture-perfect ending to that dramatic search for her, and I couldn't have imagined it coming out any better than this.

We drove through San Francisco looking around, taking in the scenery, but mostly looking for a place where we could be together in private. As we approached the business district, I recognized a sign for one of the super swanky hotels they just built out here. I pulled up in front and gave the keys to the valet, opening Aly's door and walking inside, hand in hand. I checked us into the hotel as she wandered around the very posh lounge area, smiling at the bellhop, acting like a fool in love. I smiled over at her as the receptionist ran my card, feeling those butterflies all over again.

When they gave me the key, I walked over, giving her my arm and walking her over to the elevator. I pressed the button to the top floor and looked over at her winking. She made a face like she was impressed with the penthouse suite, and I just laughed, shaking my head.

"Nothing but the best for my baby," I said in a fake rich man voice.

"Of course," she replied, pretending to smoke a cigarette.

I shook my head and pulled her close to me. She turned toward me, her lips pressed against my neck. Immediately, chills ran up and down my spine, and my cock started getting hard. The joking had stopped, and I couldn't will the elevator to go fast enough. I wanted it to hit supersonic speed, so I could take this woman, the woman I loved, and have hot crazy sex with her.

When the elevator finally rang, I let out a sigh of relief and pulled her out into the small hallway. I fumbled with the key card, trying to get it in the door, groaning as she nibbled on my earlobe. Finally, she reached down and took it from me, laughing at my inability to focus. She carefully slid the card in the box and waited until the light turned green before opening the door and ushering me inside.

The second that door closed behind us, my hands were on her, cupping her face and pressing my lips against hers. We backed into the penthouse, not even looking around, stripping clothes off one another. I stopped her in the middle of the floor and grabbed her, pulling her to me with force. I was a bit rough in my haste, but I knew she didn't care, and in fact, she was rough right back at me. We had been apart too damn long, and we were making up for all the lost time. This woman drove me absolutely wild, and all I wanted to do was taste her skin again.

I stepped back and pulled her shirt off, leaning against her and unclasping her bra. Her breasts spilled out into my hands, and I grabbed them roughly, squeezing them hard as I pushed her backward toward the bedroom. She moaned into my mouth, turning me on even more. We stopped at the foot of the bed, and she frantically fumbled with my belt. I smiled, pulling my pants down and stepping out of them. She returned the smile, undoing hers and dropping them to her feet. I licked my lips and pushed her backward on the bed, watching her bounce up and down. I reached forward and ripped her panties right off her, flinging the fabric across the room. She tried to sit up, but I wouldn't let her. Instead, I pulled off my boxer briefs and stood in front of her, stroking my cock.

She smiled and licked her lips, patting the bed next to her. I nodded and lay down, watching as she sat up on her knees and turned around, straddling my face. I groaned, immediately grabbing her by the hips and pulling that perfect, wet pussy down onto my mouth. She screamed out in pleasure, rotating her hips against my tongue. Slowly, she leaned forward and grabbed my cock in her palm stroking it up and down as she rubbed the tip against her lips. I turned my face back forth in her pussy as she lunged forward, opening wide and taking my cock all the way down her throat.

I growled into her mound, feeling her body moving over me, her top half bobbing up and down while her bottom half ground against my face. I couldn't get enough of her, of the way she tasted, the way she moved. I licked up and down her lips, sucking on her clit, feeling the vibrations of her screams against my shaft as she sucked my cock with purpose. Suddenly, she sat up straight, grabbing onto her tits and moaning loudly. I could feel her body shaking above me as she exploded in orgasm, exploding her juices all down my chin. I moaned, lapping her up until her body began to relax again. She shivered on top of me, my tongue flicking against her nub. She laughed, lifting up, but I pulled her back down, torturing her a little more before letting her go.

Instead of moving off me, she moved down me, keeping her thighs tight against me as she inched her way down toward my cock. Slowly she lowered herself down, taking me deep inside of her, riding me reverse cowgirl. I swiped my fingers down her back as she bounced up and down, looking back at me with a coy grin. She shoved her body downward and spread her thighs apart, pulling my cock all the way inside. Slowly, she began to bend over, inching her way down, grabbing onto my calves before slapping her hips up and down, over and over. I groaned, grabbing onto her ass, feeling her juices rolling down my shaft and over my balls.

She screamed out in pleasure as I slapped her ass, grabbing and jiggling it hard to take away the sting. As she slowed her hips down and rocked forward and back on my big dick, I slid my hand over and pushed a finger inside of her ass. She gasped and groaned, pushing back even farther, loving that I was filling her holes. She moaned and wailed and came almost to a stop, her pussy vibrating against my cock as I finger fucked her ass. She dug her fingernails into my calves and then started moving again, her body fully into everything I was giving her. She was close to another orgasm, and I wanted to feel it so badly.

I pulled my finger out and lifted her up, tossing her over on her back on the bed. I flipped over on top of her and leaned down, kissing her passionately on the mouth. I pushed my hand between her legs and rubbed her pussy as I swiped my tongue through her mouth. She moaned and screamed when I pushed two fingers inside of her and moved them forward and back as fast as I could.

"You gonna come for me?" I said, close to her face. "Huh?"

"Yeah," she wailed. "I wanna come on your cock."

"Oh, yeah?" I said biting her bottom lip. "You ready for it?"

"Uh-huh," she moaned.

"You sure?" I smiled. "Ask me nicely."

"Please, baby," she cried out. "Fuck me hard."

"Mmmm." I swung around and rammed my cock into her as hard as I could.

She called out, arching her chest in the air as I grabbed her waist and plowed into her over and over again. God, she was so hot, and I was having a tough time not coming. She lifted her ass off the bed, and I grabbed her by the hips, thrusting my body forward and back, groaning and moaning as her screams went higher and higher in pitch. As her back lifted off the bed, she wailed, exploding into a long, hard orgasm. I clamped my hands down on her waist, her pussy pulsating against my shaft, her hot juices flowing all over it. I took a deep breath and tilted my head back, grunting loudly as I thrust one last time and then exploded inside of her.

Our bodies stayed locked for a long time, the waves of orgasm continuing to flow through both of us. After a little while, we both collapsed, her into the bed, me down onto my knees, hanging my head toward the bed. I breathed deeply and fast, my heart beating a million miles a minute. I looked up at her as she tried to catch her breath, shaking her head and laughing.

"Holy... shit," she said breathlessly. "That was the best orgasm I've ever had."

"I might have to second that motion," I replied, putting one arm down and pulling out of her.

I collapsed onto the bed facedown next to her, relaxing as my breathing began to slow. I turned my head and saw my jacket lying on the ground, so I carefully reached down and pulled it to the side, grabbing the black box out of the front pocket. I opened the box and secretly took the ring out, laying my head back down and turning to face her. She opened her eyes and turned toward me, a huge smile on her face.

"What?" I said.

"Oh, nothing, just this handsome guy told me he loved me today," she said.

"Oh, yeah?" I smiled. "Can he tell you something else?"

"What?" She laughed, her arms on my chest.

"This." I pulled up the ring and slipped it onto her finger.

For a moment, she froze, staring at the huge, square diamond glistening on her finger. I could see a tear coming from the edge of her eye, but she sniffled and wiped it away. She cleared her throat and looked at me with attitude.

"Are you just going to put it on there, or are you going to ask first?" she said.

"Oh, I'm not asking you, baby," I said, shaking my head with a smirk. "I'm telling you. I am never letting you leave me ever again."

She smiled and leaned in, kissing me passionately on the lips. I couldn't believe it. The woman of my dreams was not only going to have my baby, but she was also going to be my wife. Sure, I had been married before, and there would always be a tiny part of me that belonged to the memory of my ex-wife, but that part of me wasn't my heart or my soul. It was my son. My heart and my soul would forever and always belong to the girl who'd blown into my life and turned it upside down. The girl who lit up the house with her magic, brought a father and a son back together, and showed me that life was so much bigger and so much more beautiful than I'd ever noticed before. I was finally getting my happy ending with a beautiful blonde nanny.

Epilogue

Aly

I stood on the hill watching the beautiful sky shimmering over the ocean. The sun was getting ready to set, and the colors that filled the clouds echoed the love in my heart. I grasped tightly to my satin-wrapped bouquet of white and roses with one lily in the center. They were just as beautiful as the ones Blake had sent me at the house in Boston a little over a year ago. My white dress fluttered wildly in the wind off the ocean, and I could see everyone taking their seats in the satin-draped chairs below in the sand. In the front row was my mother sitting next to my beautiful little girl perched in a handmade basket covered in pink silk blankets. It was the perfect scene, the perfect day to marry the man of my dreams.

"Are you ready?" my dad asked, walking up beside me and giving me his arm.

"I've never been readier." I smiled

The violinist at the front of the altar began to play Cannon in D, and the entire party of people stood to their feet and looked back as the bridesmaids made their way to the front dressed in blue silk dresses. I grasped my father's arm tightly as I made my way down the stairs and onto the sand. My bare feet sunk down into the warm ground as I smiled big, looking straight ahead at Blake, a tear falling down his cheek. As I passed the front, I stopped, reaching out to Cooper who was diligently watching his baby sister. He smiled and kissed my hand, making the whole group ooh and ah.

Cooper was the best big brother I could have ever imagined for our baby girl, Fiona. He doted over her constantly, protected her, and was completely enamored with her tender beauty. We were two very lucky people, and we were about to become one in front of all of our friends and family. All of my family was there, and so was Blake's, making a really wonderful gathering full of love and caring. My brother stood proudly next to Blake, trying to hold back tears as I looked over at him and winked. My father brought me to the front and looked up at the pastor.

"Who today will give this bride?"

"I will," my father said in a trembling voice.

I turned toward him and smiled, trying to hold my emotions together. He leaned down and kissed my cheek, whispering an "I love you" into my ear. He turned and shook Blake's hand before handing me over and stepping back to sit next to my mom. I walked forward with Blake, turning and looking deeply into his eyes. I smiled wide, shaking my head slightly and holding back the tears trying to force their way out.

The pastor went through the service, reciting several different passages from books we both loved. When it reached the time for vows, we released each other's hands and took our papers from our wedding party. I went first, trembling as I read.

"Blake, you're the most caring, strong, and amazing man I have ever met. You came into my life so unexpectedly, and though things weren't always a fairy tale, I never once stopped loving you. You're the man that I want to watch my new son turn into, the father I want to spoil our baby girl, and the husband I want to grow old with. Thank you for choosing me as your partner. I promise to love and cherish you and Cooper and Fiona for the rest of my life."

The pastor turned to Blake who was already struggling not to cry. It was the first time I had ever seen him this emotional, and it made my heart almost leap from my chest. I had never had someone love me so much.

"Aly, you jumped into our life like lightning from the sky. You blew through like a hurricane, only instead of bringing destruction, you mended so many broken bridges. You pulled my heart from the floor, sewed it back together, and gave me a new purpose in life. You took my son and showed him the love he'd once lost. You renewed us, and you continue to do that every day. You're the mother of my daughter and now of my son, and there isn't a person on this earth better fit for that job. I promise to love you, cherish you, and stand by your side for the rest of my life."

I wiped the tears flowing down my cheek and handed my paper back to my sister. The pastor reached his hand out and opened it, revealing two perfect wedding bands. His was solid gold, our initials etched on the outside. Mine was silver, a pair of wings carefully sculpted and overlapping like the wings of a dove. He took mine first and carefully pushed it onto my finger, picking up my hand and pressing his lips to it. I did the same, grasping it tightly in mine as we turned back and looked at the pastor.

"By the solemn powers vested in me by this great state of California, I now pronounce you husband and wife," the pastor said, smiling. "You may now kiss the bride."

I smiled and stepped forward into his arms, pressing my lips firmly against his. My heart was so full, and I couldn't help weeping, standing there in the beautiful setting sun. I wrapped my arms around his neck and kissed him harder until my father faked a cough from the audience, and the whole place went up in laughter and cheers. It was the most beautiful moment of my life.

After the ceremony, we went up to the tent on the beach set up for the wedding party. I changed out of my very expensive gown into a simple white, long summer dress so I could hold Fiona. Blake changed, too, taking off his tux and hanging it on the hanger next to my dress and pulling on a pair of board shorts, a loose cotton button-down, and some flip-flops. He walked over and stared into my eyes.

"I love you," he said with a smile.

"I love you too," I said with a giggle.

We left the tent and made our way out to the enclosed area of the beach where we had tables set up, covered in candles with a bonfire to the side and a dance floor in the middle. The band was already playing, and people were dancing when we got down there. It was the perfect party with the perfect amount of light and the roar of laughter and love from our families. I walked over to my mother and kissed her on the head, looking over at Fiona sleeping soundly despite the loud music from the DJ. I swore that girl could sleep through anything, just like her father.

Blake and I took our seats with the wedding party and ate dinner, a wonderful feast of shrimp, crab, and steaks. It was exactly what Blake wanted, and everyone really enjoyed themselves. When we were done with dinner, we cut the cake and then excused ourselves to the tent to say goodbye to my mother and father. My mom picked Fiona up out of the basket and smiled, turning and handing her over to me. I looked down at her sweet blue eyes and curly blond hair, and my heart just melted. My mother was going to be keeping her for the weekend for us so we could have a quick honeymoon before we started the entire process of moving. It was going to be the first time I was away from her for more than a couple of hours.

My heart was breaking just thinking about not waking up to feed her in the morning. Still, it was important that we had our time together, and Cooper was going to be staying there, too, just to keep an eye on his sister. I picked Fiona up in the air and kissed her chubby little cheeks, bringing her in and hugging her gently. I walked over to Blake who was saying goodbye to Cooper and switched with him. He walked away with Fiona, and I bent down in front of Cooper, straightening his bow tie.

"You looked so handsome tonight," I said.

"You were so beautiful," he said. "I just want to tell you I'm happy you're going to be my mom now. I know my mom would be proud to have a woman like you there for me."

"You are so sweet," I said, breaking into tears again. "And so grown-up. Gosh. Come here, give me a hug. You take care of Fiona for me, okay? And don't eat too many cookies. Grandma loves to bake cookies."

"I'll show her how to make those ones we invented," he said.

"Yes, good idea," I said, ruffling his hair. "I'll miss you."

"I'll miss you too," he said, hugging me tightly once again.

We waved goodbye to them as they drove off, and Blake hugged me tightly, knowing I was going to have a hard time being without them. There was going to be so many changes coming up, and we were moving our whole life out to California after the honeymoon. We wanted Cooper to finish out the school year in Boston, and it took some time for Blake to convince his investors that moving the company to Cali was a good business move, but finally, we were ready to take the leap. Boston was great, and it had a very special place in my heart, but with the baby and becoming a family, we both wanted to be close to our families.

Cooper was super excited to move out to San Francisco, especially since he would get to be part of two very loving families. Out in Boston, it was just him and his dad until I came around, and I could tell he needed that extra support from them. He had his room packed before we were able to touch anything else in the house.

We went back to the party for a couple more hours and then were ushered off by limo to catch our flight. We were jetting off to the islands for a couple of days to catch some more sun and relaxation. I had never been to the islands before, so I was really excited. I was pretty sure Blake was in it for the nookie since we never got any time away from the kids. I had to admit, I didn't pack that many clothes, not expecting to be wearing them for most of the trip.

When we got to the airport, they were just boarding first class, so we checked in and headed on board. As we moved through the aisles, waiting for the people in front of us to stow their luggage, Blake leaned down and whispered softly in my ear.

"You know, we could totally make this another first and join the mile-high club," he said, pinching my butt. "It's totally doable from first class."

I laughed, moving forward and climbing into our seats. He leaned in and kissed me hard, pulling away and smiling big. I fastened my seatbelt and looked out the window, watching as the plane left the ground. A year before, I was walking into his home, not knowing what to expect, thinking all I would gain was the ability to finish my degree. It was crazy what could happen in a year. We had a baby, got married, and now, we were headed off to our honeymoon. Blake was the man of my dreams, the man I never thought I would end up with. After all that time, I had finally gotten my happily ever after.

The End